Cynthia

D0191019

SpringSong Books

Carrie

Cynthia

Jenny

Kara

Lisa

Michelle

Cynthia

Leila Prince Golding

BETHANY HOUSE PUBLISHERS
MINNEAPOLIS, MINNESOTA 55438

Cynthia
Leila Prince Golding

Library of Congress Catalog Card Number 94–27174

ISBN 1–55661–524–8

Published by Bethany House Publishers
A Ministry of Bethany Fellowship, Inc.
11300 Hampshire Avenue South
Minneapolis, Minnesota 55438

Printed in the United States of America

Dedicated to

my daughter

Kathleen Golding Carlson,

Mother of the Cynthia

for whom this book was written

Acknowledgments

For background and thoughts,
sincere thanks go to
Clarissie Carroll
of
Mitchell, Indiana,
who served for years
as
The Lady in the Tower.

Sincere appreciation also to Juanita Bennett and Florence Hortsman of the Henry Schricker Library for their assistance with research, and to Michael Ellis, Beverly Stout, and Ken Gregory of the Indiana Department of Natural Resources.

1

Dark, ominous clouds rolled up over the southern edge of the horizon as the sun sank behind the pine trees. From her high perch in the fire tower, Cynthia Carlson watched the clouds expand like spilled ink, blotting out the glint of the early stars and the faint illumination of the sickle moon. She shivered slightly.

"What an initiation," Cyndi whispered to herself. The awesome sight gave her an intense feeling of solitude as her brown eyes carefully scanned the darkening ocean of treetops surrounding her. The earlier whisper of dying breeze had suddenly swelled to a distant rustling in the pines, maples, and cottonwoods far below her tiny cabin. Poised a hundred feet in the air on four spindly looking steel legs, the seven-foot-square room seemed to Cyndi like an eagle's nest high on a mountain ledge.

I'm more alone than I've ever been, she thought, gazing ruefully around her tiny nest. Tears began to fill Cyndi's eyes, but she brushed them resolutely away. She reminded herself this was what she had wanted—to get away from friends, from memories, from Mark. Most of all from Mark, from the possibility of a chance meeting with him. She couldn't face that, not for a while at least.

Concern darkened her eyes as distant thunder rumbled and spears of lightning jabbed through the blackness of the farthest clouds. A few tentative drops of rain tapped on the metal roof. Hurriedly, Cyndi swung the windows shut and turned to finish her evening duties.

Several intermittent splats of rain hit the window she had just closed, and she recalled the chief forest ranger's warning: "Don't stay in the fire tower during a storm." She didn't want to test the validity of his statement.

Stepping to the four-foot-high metal cabinet in the middle of the little room, Cyndi removed the weather log from its daytime spot and wrote an entry on one of the lined pages.

Raindrops were drumming steadily on the metal roof now. She quickly bent and reached into the cabinet for the psychrometer. Carefully she slipped it and the weather log into a weatherproof tote beside her empty canteen for the trip home and tomorrow's early reading.

Placing the radio inside the small iron box on which it had been sitting, Cyndi locked the box, stood, and made a final check of the area through the wide windows encompassing the little room. Deep thunder rolled as lightning crackled ominously, splitting the black sky above her in jagged lines.

As Cyndi grabbed her tote and reached down for the trapdoor at one side of the room, heavy gusts of wind began shaking the fire tower. Lifting the cumbersome door, she let it rest on her back as her feet reached for the steps below, then let the door fall shut behind her. The strength of the wind surprised her. She grabbed the railings tightly, trying to resist the powerful gust that tore at her as she descended the steps of the first flight.

"Only another hundred and fifteen to go, Cinder," she told herself as she reached the first landing, her hands gripping the wet, slippery metal of the handrails.

Although uneasy about the slippery stairs, she smiled as she recalled her childhood enchantment with the image of Cinderella descending the palace stairs, and her brother David's antagonistic name-calling: Cinder Carlson. But she had become even angrier when during high school, he suggested her boyfriend Mark was not the prince she had hoped for. Regret now overcame her as she realized David had been right. Angry with herself, she forced her thoughts back to the task at hand—getting safely down to the ground from this high, scary place.

Above her the tower was shaking and rattling with increased momentum as the wind rose and tore around with almost gale-like force. The rain, coming down in torrents, had Cyndi's curly blond hair and khaki uniform soaked by the time she was halfway down the seemingly endless flights of dark, rain-slicked stairs. Shivering uncontrollably, she felt great relief when her feet finally touched the ground; she realized she had been holding her breath down the last slippery flight.

Cyndi peered across the clearing through the pelting, blowing rain to the dark shape that was her car, then rushed toward it, slipped inside, and slammed the door. As she tossed her tote on the passenger seat, she felt the water dribble from her knees to her sopping wet shoes. For a few moments she sat huddled with her hands gripping her shoulders trying to stop shaking. Finally able to turn the key in the ignition, she backed into a small turnabout, then headed through the sheets of rain, slowly, carefully down the narrow road between towering trees that led to the highway.

The driving rain forced her to maneuver slowly so she wouldn't miss the crossroads and her turnoff. She sighed with relief when she finally reached the familiar drive that led to Grandpa Carlson's Victorian farmhouse. She sensed a warm welcome, a feeling of comfort in the cold, wet darkness when she peered through the driving rain and saw the glow of the automatic porch light.

Later, her pants and shirt dripping from a line on the back porch, Cyndi, dressed in her grandfather's worn, gray robe, stood at a kitchen window towel-drying her hair as she brooded over the bad weather. She wished Ace hadn't flown to Indianapolis that day, but he had made the trip seem important. Now his lateness worried her; he should have returned well before the weather turned bad. She hoped he hadn't started out, but considering his usual self-confidence, she suspected he had tried to beat the storm.

Cyndi's thoughts drifted back to that morning. Soon after she had climbed the fire tower, opening a few windows to admit the spring air, Ace had phoned. "Cyndi, I have to fly to Indianapolis today," he had announced. "How about a picnic this evening if I get back in time? I'll bring the fixings, you bring the blanket and paper plates. What do you say?" His deep, now familiar voice had sounded happy, full of fun.

"I'd love to, Tim."

Cyndi had imagined his smile as he talked, the unruly lock of dark brown hair that perpetually fell over his broad brow, the tiny smile-wrinkles at the corners of his eyes. They had chatted easily for several minutes. She felt comfortable talking with the young man she knew both as Tim and Ace.

But later in the morning she had noticed the little pearly clouds had disappeared, replaced by other small white ones scattered across the blue expanse. Soon those had begun giving way to longer, thicker clouds. In the early afternoon they had looked like white towers in the azure sky.

"That could develop into something nasty," Cyndi had mumbled, removing the psychrometer from the cabinet and climbing down to the ground to take another reading.

Adjusting a tiny, dampened gauze stocking over the bulb of one of the two glass thermometers mounted on the metal base, she had faced into the wind and twirled the psychrometer on its handle for a minute. After quickly reading both bulbs, she had recorded the figures and climbed back to the cabin to calculate the danger of fire.

Throughout the afternoon the clouds had heaped into large shapes, towering ever higher. Cyndi had marveled as some of them mushroomed like giant-capped souffles fresh from the oven, reminding her of the unbelievable power the grand, darkening panorama held; the potential for thunder and lightning and damaging winds. Now, from Grandpa's kitchen, she watched the spectacle in safety as she pushed damp curls back from her forehead and tightened the sash on Grandpa's large robe. Her brow wrinkled with concern for Tim as she stepped toward the screened porch to hang her towel beside her dripping uniform. The phone rang before she was finished.

Throwing the towel in a soggy lump over the makeshift line, she raced back through the kitchen and into the living room. Poised on the edge of Grandpa's leather chair, she snatched the receiver.

"Tim?" she asked a bit breathlessly.

"Hi, Cyndi—how'd you know?"

"Lucky, I guess . . ."

"Say, the cloud ceiling was getting too low, so I decided to stay over until tomorrow. How are things there?"

Cyndi slid back into the big chair.

"It's storming quite hard. I just came in a few minutes ago, soaking wet."

"You must have looked like a half-drowned poodle with that tousled hair of yours," Tim chuckled.

"I suppose I did. This isn't exactly picnic weather."

"Yeah. About our picnic, we'd better take a rain check until the weekend—and no pun intended."

Cyndi was silent for a moment, disappointment and an out-of-proportion sense of loneliness washing over her.

"Aren't you coming back until then?" she asked.

"Well, after the heavy rain there, I won't have to be in the tower for several days. I'll call you when I get back."

"Okay, Ace," Cyndi answered, an edge of disappointment in her voice. "Bye." She slumped into the massive chair and stared blankly at the darkness outside the window.

After a few moments, she pushed herself out of the comfort of the chair and went to the kitchen. Getting milk and eggs from the refrigerator, she made an omelet for supper and sat at the round oak table to eat it and drink a glass of milk.

"I can't understand why I'm so disappointed," she mumbled. "After all, it was only a picnic. I suppose I'm getting lonesome from the isolation, and it does sometimes get eerie being alone without Grandpa all the time in this big old house, nice as it is."

Then, being honest with herself, Cyndi realized that Tim's voice and soft blue eyes had been in her thoughts a lot the past few weeks. She knew, too, that probably had a lot to do with her disappointment at the cancellation of their date.

She really didn't want him on her mind so much, didn't think she wanted *any* man to assume importance in her life right now. Mark had been more than enough for a while.

I don't intend to think about him, either, she thought sullenly. *He took up too much of my time and thoughts during high school. Then to come home from my first semester at college and find him married!*

Cyndi washed her few dishes, then went into the living room to curl up in the old brown-leather chair with the novel she had started reading the previous evening for Literature credit.

Heavy rain continued to pound on the roof and lash against the windows as Cyndi tried to absorb herself in her book. But Tim kept pushing his way into her thoughts, try as she would to keep him out. Finally laying the novel aside, she pulled a faded blue afghan around her shoulders, letting her reflections return to the days just before she met him.

Grandpa had written to her at college asking that she spend her spring break with him, so she had cancelled plans for a short visit to her roommate's home.

Grandpa had appeared older than she remembered him from Christmas when he was with her and David at their aunt's home. His eyes were still bright and happy beneath his wavy gray hair, but his step seemed to have slowed a lot.

At breakfast the first morning of her visit, he reminded her of her childhood dream of one day manning the fire tower as he did, and asked if she would like to do it now.

"Climb the tower with *you*?" she asked incredulously. "Wouldn't that be too tiring for you, Grandpa?"

"Probably would be, honey," he said. "These old legs are too contrary lately when it comes to climbing anything higher than the front porch. No, I meant, how would you feel about manning the fire tower, taking the job for the spring and summer?"

"Grandpa, you're not serious," she laughed.

"Sure am," he said. "Fellow who had the job decided to move to another state near some kinfolk, and no one's been found to take his place. But I never forgot what you said as a little tyke."

Grandpa took a bite of his toast and chewed while she considered the suggestion. "Then, I'll do it!" she answered brightly. "When do I start?"

"Soon as possible. Ace has been trying to fit this tower in with the schedule he already has on the one over at Walnut Ridge."

"Ace?"

"Timothy Nichols; lives about ten miles from here. With the towers and trying to keep his dad's farm going while his hip is mending, Ace really has his hands full," Grandpa explained.

"I'll have to check when I get back to school, but my grades have been exceptionally good." She looked thoughtfully out the window. "Maybe I can cut out the rest of the semester classes and get credit for independent study and taking exams by fall."

"I'll give Ace a call," Grandpa said, smiling as though he was especially pleased with himself. "Maybe he can come by this evening and fill you in on what to expect. Been years since I worked up there. Helping to fight a fire now would wear me to a frazzle."

"If his name's Timothy, why do you call him Ace?" Cyndi asked.

Chuckling, Grandpa tried to explain. "When Tim was just a little fellow, he became quite taken with the thought of flying. Was always making model planes. Said he was going to be an

A–1 pilot when he grew up—what we called a flying ace in my day. His family and I have called him Ace ever since."

"Did he become a pilot?"

"Sure did! He worked hard as a youngster, soon's he was old enough. Took every odd job he could get and saved most every penny for flying lessons. Got his pilot's license at age seventeen. He's a fine young man," Grandpa added, looking sideways at her.

The weeks following that evening had passed swiftly, with arrangements at the college followed by training for the new job. Now, after her first day on tower duty, Cyndi was glad she'd accepted the challenge. Even with today's storm, she knew she was going to enjoy it.

She yawned, pushed the afghan off her shoulders, and ran her fingers through her still-damp curls. She picked up the novel, then put it aside again, deciding she didn't feel like reading; she was restless.

The rain was no longer pelting the windows so viciously, indicating the wind had dropped somewhat. She padded across the linoleum-covered floor in her bare feet and opened the front door. Rain fell steadily, though more muted now. She felt sure it would stop by morning.

Cyndi woke to sunshine streaming beneath the partially rolled shade, the sweet scent of lilacs wafting through the slit of opened window. A few drops of leftover rain plopped from the eaves. As Tim had said, there was little need to man the towers after the soaking rain, so dressing in a pair of old jeans and sneakers, she stuffed a couple of apples in her jacket pockets and got a small basket from the pantry. She would search for something special for her evening meal.

Slipping the handle over her arm, she left the house by the back door, walked past the rarely used water pump where bees were investigating lemon-thyme, down the path toward a field of ancient fruit trees; Grandpa had said his constant pruning kept them bearing, and they were in blossom now.

Cyndi strolled along, kicking gently at the brown leaves of last autumn, watching robins eagerly pulling at worms in areas of greening grass, then stopping a minute as a gray-brown rabbit hopped out of her way into a small brush pile when she entered the orchard.

"Ah, there's one." Stepping over a short length of rotting log, she bent and picked a light brown cone-shaped object, its color blending well with the surroundings. She inhaled the cool scent, which reminded her of clean, damp, just-turned earth. By the time she headed back to the house, the small basket was half full of morrel mushrooms, their surfaces cool and moist under the damp ferns she'd used to cover them.

"What a supper I'm going to have," she said to herself. "Wish Grandpa was here; he relishes mushrooms braised in butter with freshly ground pepper."

Pausing at the asparagus bed running along the edge of the backyard, she stooped and snapped off a few fat spears close to the ground, putting them on top of the ferns.

Cyndi glanced up to follow the call of a cardinal high in the oak tree; her glance took in a flash of red-gold where the sun's rays hit an upstairs window. It vividly reminded her of the fiery dream and the real possibility of having to fight a fire in circumstances more frightening than those she had faced in training. She shuddered, hoping she hadn't taken a job she couldn't handle. Then mentally shaking herself, confident of the training she'd had, she continued across the yard, determined to enjoy the day.

On the day of their rescheduled picnic, Tim arrived early in the evening with a bouquet of fragrant purple lilacs.

"Tim, how sweet!" Cyndi exclaimed, marveling at the abundance of flowerettes in each bloom.

In the kitchen, Cyndi arranged the stiff, woody-stemmed flowers in a squat yellow bowl before setting out with Tim to their favorite picnic spot.

Later as they ate the sandwiches Cyndi had packed, Tim commented on the wariness in her eyes. "You seem to be pulling away from me, Cyndi."

"I guess I'm trying to get over the pain of a broken relationship," Cyndi answered with a small, humorless laugh. "I cared about someone more than he cared about me. At least I thought he was important to me. I'm realizing now perhaps he'd just become a habit, part of my social life. Anyway," she added, tossing her head, "that's all in the past. I try not to think about it."

"Sometimes talking about it removes some of the pain," Tim offered.

"Actually, the hurt part is pretty much gone. I think I'm more angry at him than anything else," she added sheepishly.

"Something like that happened to me during my last year at college," Tim stated, "so I can understand how you feel." He smiled gently at her, his blue eyes sincere in their warmth of offered friendship. "Now, let's both put those bad times behind us and not think about them anymore. We'll just enjoy our time together. Okay?"

"Okay," Cyndi answered, taking the hand he offered. He pulled her up from where she sat on the edge of the picnic blanket and they strolled together down an almost obliterated path to the site of an old gristmill, its rough gray surface almost covered with vines of ivy and Virginia creeper, the foundation obscured by masses of ferns. "It's so pretty," she said, stopping near the edge of the stream that rushed over the remains of a large water wheel.

"Becomes even nicer as the seasons go on," Tim commented, helping her across slippery, mossy stones and onto a narrow footbridge that sturdily belied its years, crossing the water to a spot near the mill's entrance. There in a patch of sunlight, white narcissus bloomed like stars among the overgrown grass.

As they walked around the mill through knee-high weeds, Tim continued his comment. "I've always thought this would make a restful, scenic location for a home." Cyndi thought about that on their stroll back to the picnic spot and heartily agreed.

Later, saying good-night at her front steps, he asked, "How's your grandfather enjoying his visit with his sister in Wisconsin?"

"Fine," Cyndi answered, laughing lightly. "Said the fishing's so great he may stay until winter—at least as long as I'll remain to care for his few chickens."

Waving to Tim as he backed his old Volkswagen van out onto the road, she listened intently to the peeping chorus of tiny tree frogs and the sweet call of an evening hawk—melodies he'd identified for her before leaving.

By early May, the weather had turned very dry, with only occasional rain. Because folks living near the forest's edge were sometimes careless with spring clean-up burning, sudden winds scattered fires, causing a lot of tension. Fortunately, not much damage occurred.

"I'm thankful none has erupted in my area yet," Cyndi told Grandpa the evening he phoned.

"Don't worry, honey; you'd handle everything fine," he assured, his voice sounding garbled because of a poor connection. "I've got confidence in you."

Cyndi, too, had confidence in herself, but she couldn't shake the sense of uneasiness that came over her when she thought of being actively involved in dealing with a roaring fire.

2

Cyndi had been spending full days in the tower, taking her lunch and canteen with her, also her textbooks.

She was enjoying a sense of peace and solitude that day, sitting at an open window surveying the scene spread out before her. From far below she could hear the singing and chirping of myriads of birds in their chosen nesting places in the trees and thickets of hawthorn and wild raspberries surrounding her quarter acre of tower grass.

The air is so calm, she thought. *Considering notations in the weather book, I'm sure there won't be any fires.*

Scooting the tall chair back from the window so the sun's glare would be out of her eyes, she started a letter to David. Describing her work, sharing Grandpa's plans, and inquiring about David's wedding scheduled for autumn, she ended by asking if he'd heard from their parents, wondering if they could possibly leave their missionary work in Mexico to attend the wedding.

When Cyndi lifted her gaze from the sheet of paper to glance outside, she saw a faint wisp of smoke. At least it appeared to be smoke, though barely discernible in the distance.

Grabbing her binoculars, she leaned on the windowsill, focusing them carefully. "It *is* smoke," she decided. Putting the binoculars on the chair, she quickly stepped to the surveying telescope where it was mounted on tracks on top of the cabinet in the center of the room. Her heart beat faster as she carefully sighted the crosshairs on the smoke.

Because the fire was too far away to determine its exact position, she hurried to pass the information on to the next tower for help in verifying the location. Kneeling on one knee, she dialed the phone, the receiver ready at her ear. *Come on, Ace, answer! Hurry up!* She was replacing the receiver after the twentieth ring when she heard his voice. "Hello, Walnut Ridge." He sounded breathless. "Sorry, I was below."

"It's Redbud tower. I need your help in positioning a possible fire!"

"Okay, Cyndi. Give me your figures, then hang on."

The minutes seemed like an hour as she waited impatiently for his clarification. "It's in the northeast section of Center Township. I've alerted Bluebird tower over the radio and we got a perfect fix. He's concerned the blaze may get out of hand around the large number of homes in that area; could cause some real problems."

Cyndi could see that the tiny plume of smoke had already grown and was definitely from a fire.

"Thanks for calling," Tim said. "I was cutting the grass; the extra time before I got back up here might have been crucial. Hey, want me to bring my mower over one day soon and help you with your area?"

"No thanks, Tim. Grandpa's old push-mower works fine."

"Okay then, bye for now. Best keep our lines clear in case they need to reach us."

"Think we'll have to help fight this one?" she asked.

"Probably not."

But Cyndi watched incredulously as the smoke, instead of diminishing, began to develop into big clouds in low billows on the far area of the forest.

She became very uneasy during the next few hours as she watched the smoking cloud expand, but hoped it was the earlier smoke spreading out on the air currents. When Tim phoned a short while later, she knew for sure. "I'm heading over there, Cyndi," he said urgently. "They need another man."

"But, Tim! I don't understand how the fire could grow so quickly on such a quiet day."

"Once it gains headway, a big fire can create its own draft. I'll call you when I get back."

"I'll be waiting; please be careful."

However, because Tim hadn't contacted her by six that evening, the usual time of leaving the tower for the day, she decided to wait an hour longer. Throughout the day she had watched the smoke spread over an ever-widening area; now she felt sure the fire had also.

Finally, about seven-thirty, she drove home, ate a light supper, and tried to study. The phone still hadn't rung by eleven when she went upstairs to prepare for bed. She was tense as she slipped under the covers, tossing and turning before finally falling asleep.

The morning dawned cool and appeared cloudy. Cyndi leisurely stretched before rising, then thought, *Oh, no! Maybe it isn't normal cloud cover, but smoke; the fire could still be burning!* She was hurriedly slipping into her robe when the phone rang.

"Cyndi?"

"Yes, Ace. You sound terrible; are you all right?"

"Just hoarse from the smoke—and tired. Just got in."

"You were fighting the fire all night?" she asked.

"Until after midnight. For a long time we couldn't seem to beat fast enough or get the backfires ahead of it . . . it kept moving in unlikely directions, but they're finally containing it. Some of us stayed to help keep watch over the little breakouts."

"Where are you now?" Cyndi asked.

"Home. I'm bushed. Fortunately it looks as though we may get a few rain showers later."

"Good. Try to get some rest."

"That shouldn't be too difficult," Tim laughed. "Goodnight—or good morning."

Cyndi smiled gently as she heard the click of his receiver. *He sounds exhausted*, she thought.

Pulling on a sweater and jeans, she went into the kitchen to start breakfast. It could simmer on the stove while she tended to Grandpa's few outside chores. She tried to avoid the large glossy, rusty-red rooster who had crowed lustily earlier and was strutting around the fenced run.

Cyndi replenished the grain and water containers under the overhang of the little chicken house and scattered a bit of straw over the litter on the floor inside, deciding to gather the eggs after she'd eaten.

The warm, nutty aroma of oatmeal and the fragrance of perking coffee met her nostrils when she opened the kitchen door, reminding her of the occasional mornings she had spent here as a child. Grandma had always prepared hot oatmeal with raisins for her and David, along with mugs of cocoa and marshmallows. Grandpa insisted they have the marshmallows, even though Grandma thought them too sweet for so early in the day.

Cyndi smiled, remembering, grateful for the pleasant memories of her grandparents.

After getting the eggs from the henhouse, she spent the early morning hours weeding the various flower beds around the large yard, then came inside to her ever-waiting studies. It was so damp outside she wouldn't go to the fire tower.

As she concentrated on reading and taking notes, a different line of thought kept running through her mind, a thought that had been bothering her off and on for the past few weeks.

Not certain why she felt this way, she found herself questioning whether she should continue this direction of study next year. *I decided years ago; why should I change my mind now?* she wondered.

There had never seemed to be quite enough money. She remembered her parents' concern every month when statements were due. Money took on a great importance—not that they coveted it for its own sake. Even as a child Cyndi knew her Christian parents weren't like that, for they both worked at extra jobs in order to honor the Lord by taking care of obligations. But accumulating interest on credit had snowballed when there wasn't enough work.

Cyndi had promised herself then that she would do whatever she could so she would have plenty of money when she became an adult. Because she had read a newspaper account of a woman in her early thirties with a six-figure annual income, working in a section of the computer industry, she had headed in that direction.

But recently, confusing thoughts about that decision were making her uneasy. Cyndi shifted restlessly on her chair. Something else had been bothering her, too, in recent weeks; the consciousness that she was neglecting something important. She knew she hadn't studied her Bible lately—hadn't even read a little from it during the past few months. It had been an important part of her daily schedule for years, ever since she had, as a little girl, asked Jesus to come into her heart.

What's the matter with me? Cyndi pondered. *Why did the spiritual part of my life change so drastically? I didn't stop reading the Scriptures and praying on purpose; at least I don't think I did.*

She put her pen down and sat looking past the bowl of lilacs, out the window between starched white curtains, not really seeing the flame-colored cardinal perched on the branch of the little redbud tree.

Cyndi had a faraway look in her brown eyes as she propped her chin in her hand, her elbow on the table. *When did I change? I guess it was right after I learned about Mark's marriage. Was I blaming God for my hurt? Did I wonder why He had let that happen to me?*

Cyndi found herself considering the direction of her life goals and wondered occasionally about Tim's ambitions, something they'd never discussed. Since she was sort of missing him anyway, she decided to invite him for a midafternoon dinner.

Over the phone she said, "When I was gathering eggs this morning, I found a rooster with his head caught between the fencepost and wire—a fine position for killing easily and quickly." She gave a small laugh. "I wanted to call and have you do the deed, but I got it done okay. Fortunately, during a weekend visit to a friend's farm home last year I was taught how to prepare a chicken for cooking. Can I interest you in a dinner around two o'clock? Your dad's invited, too."

"He's having an old friend here for lunch and an afternoon of checkers and crop-talk. Okay if I come alone?"

"Of course," Cyndi laughed. "Be hungry."

They were finishing off the meal with custard pie when she said, "Tim, you mentioned once that you'd graduated from Purdue but didn't say what you majored in. Were you preparing for something specific?"

"Mainly for Dad's sake, I wanted to learn as much as I could about modern agricultural methods," he explained. "But my desire has always been to be a naturalist in some capacity, so I crammed in all the subjects on both that I could handle. Since then I've been using the library to continue studying natural science."

Cyndi gave a small nod, her brown eyes pensive. The things of nature had definitely caught her interest since she'd been in this area. She guessed she had never taken time to notice the absolute wonder of it before. Then, too, her growing realization of God's rightful place in her life, His priorities, had given her a different outlook on things.

Tim's voice broke into her thoughts. "Angela, the girl I was dating, tried to steer me in a money-making direction with her father's large trucking company. To tell you the truth, I strongly considered it—against my better judgment."

"Why didn't you take it?" Cyndi couldn't mask her curiosity.

"A verse from Isaiah kept coming to my mind," Tim answered. " 'Everyone that is called by my name, I have created for my glory.' "

"Couldn't you have been a witness for the Lord there as well as anywhere else?" she questioned.

"Probably could have," Tim responded thoughtfully. "It would certainly have produced a fine salary with plenty to give for God's work, but I figured He may have given me naturalist instincts for some specific work in His plan that I hadn't discovered yet. Anyway, I turned the offer down."

"Is that when Angela dropped you?" Cyndi asked bluntly.

Tim nodded. "It hurt at first, but I haven't regretted the decision. Anyone would welcome a lot of money, but some folks find greater happiness in humble positions—humble in the world's eyes, I mean. No job is too humble if it's honest, and I'm happy working here and able to make a decent living."

Cyndi was still debating his statement so she said nothing. Tim began to share with her the interest his Sunday school kids were taking in learning about God's care for them through illustrations from nature.

After Tim had left for home, she cleaned the kitchen, her mind on Tim's decisiveness about his life's goals and the girl he'd been dating. Cyndi knew she, too, needed to make a definite recommitment of her life to the Lord.

When Cyndi had put the last dish away, she went to the open window, relishing the soft coolness of the breeze laden this late afternoon with the perfume of violets and a faint scent of early strawberries.

"I'm sorry, Lord," she whispered, tears filling her eyes and sliding down her cheeks. "Forgive me for being so foolish, allowing myself to fall in love with Mark without asking you about it."

She brushed the tears away and went upstairs to sit on the edge of her bed. This room, too, held memories of visits during her childhood—memories warm with the loving care and enjoyment of her grandparents.

Cyndi's thoughts of the past twined together with the present as her hand brushed across the tufted white bedspread she was sitting on. Her gaze moved over the polished wood floor, bare except for the thick, hand-braided rug beside the bed, so well remembered from those times.

Even the rose-flowered, ivy-twined wallpaper was the same. So were the long, crocheted runners on the dresser and chest of drawers. She reached over to run her hand along the back of the child-sized rocker that still held a well-worn teddy bear dressed in a blue stocking cap.

Picking up her small leather-covered Bible, Cyndi carried it to the window, slid the sash all the way open, and sat on the floor beneath it to read. The breeze, saturated with sweetness from the lilacs on the giant bush just outside, ruffled the soft curls at her temples.

Opening the little book, Cyndi slowly turned the delicate pages, not sure where she wanted to start reading. Flipping through it randomly, her eyes fell on parts of verse eight in Psalm 5.

Lord lead me . . .
Tell me clearly what to do,
Which way to turn.

She continued to turn the pages, letting her gaze run over the verses, occasionally stopping to read one. She was about to close the book when she saw the first part of Psalm 138:8; it seemed just for her.

The Lord will work out

His plans for my life.

"Thank you, God," she whispered. "Thank you for caring about me and the decisions in my life. And thank you for reminding me."

Cyndi turned to the beginning pages of the New Testament then and began reading, marveling that the story seemed brand new even though she had read it many times.

An hour or so later she stood, stretched, and put her Bible on the nightstand, deciding to go for a walk.

Stopping in the kitchen, she peeled an onion and stuck a few cloves in it before slipping it into the kettle of beans soaking on the stove. After dropping in a few bay leaves and turning the flame low, she slipped a handful of peanuts into her shirt pocket and went out the back door.

She crossed the yard to the big oak tree at the corner. Pods like tiny beige propellers twirled from high branches where pink-tinged clusters were beginning to open into new green leaves. A pair of golden-brown baby squirrels left the cavity in the tree and crept warily out on a limb.

Cyndi had walked through a wooded area and fields dotted with wildflowers when she glanced at her watch and, noting the time, headed back in the direction of the house, returning by a different route. She strolled through a secluded area where a small stream moved through a group of willows and emerging cattails then flowed over a scattered rockbed with a pleasant tinkling like a wind chime. *The perfect spot for a picnic,* she thought.

Her contemplation was abruptly interrupted when, glancing up, she saw two men standing at the far edge of the next pasture beside what appeared to be a State Police car. Their backs were toward her, but as one of them partially turned, it looked as though he was scanning the area with binoculars.

Startled, Cyndi dropped to her knees.

"Why am I afraid?" she scolded herself. "I haven't done anything wrong." But she continued to crouch there, peering through the brambles of a blackberry bush.

"Why would the police be concerned with Grandpa's land?" she speculated. "What are they suspicious about?" For reasons she couldn't fathom, Cyndi had a sense of foreboding.

She crept around the edge of the field. Staying within the shadows of the trees at the forest's edge, she circled around to where she was quite close to them and could see without being seen.

They were preparing to get into their car and Cyndi could see them clearly. Both were fairly young, of medium height with muscular build; but there the similarity ended.

She watched as the nice-looking blond one got in on the driver's side. The officer who slid into the passenger's seat was one of the handsomest men she had ever seen. Probably Hispanic, she thought, since his skin was light brown and he had flashing black eyes and hair the shade of polished ebony.

They were officers of the law; she should feel safe around them. Yet as she walked back to the house, she could not shake the feeling of apprehension that clouded the remainder of the day.

3

The next morning, Sunday, was bright with sunshine and singing birds when Cyndi awoke.

Remembering her resolve to not neglect the Lord's rightful place in her life, she decided to start going to church, which she had failed to do recently.

Going downstairs in her robe and slippers, she went to Grandpa's room and got the church bulletin he had left on his dresser for her.

Finding the time of the morning service, she checked her watch, noting that she had just enough time to get ready without having to rush.

The church, a small, white clapboard building with a tall, slender steeple, stood just within a grove of pine trees at the edge of town.

As Cyndi parked her car and got out, the bell began ringing a welcome to the worship service.

Cyndi received warm handshakes from several people before she slipped quietly into a pew. As the congregation began singing, a lady near her handed her a hymnbook.

When the choir began singing, she glanced at the little child seated beside her, a dark-haired girl of about three who looked up at her with a cherubic grin and the offer of a tiny stuffed doll. Cyndi gave her a smile, then exchanged one with the attractive young woman seated on the other side of the child.

Her lovely, long black hair and large, dark eyes reminded

Cyndi of someone, but she couldn't recall who it was.

Following the closing prayer, the young woman reached out her hand and introduced herself.

"I'm Carlita Hernandez; this is my daughter Luz. And my husband, Al," she added, turning to the bearded man beside her, who appeared to be in his late thirties.

"Cynthia Carlson," she responded, taking their hands in turn.

"Are you perhaps part of the family of David Carlson?" Al asked.

"Yes. He's my grandfather. I have a brother, David, also. Do you know my grandfather?"

"Yes, since Carlita and I moved here some years ago," Al said. "Our families lived in Texas for many years following our grandparents' immigration from Mexico."

"Where is your grandfather?" Carlita asked. "Is he not well? And, may I ask, where is the rest of your family?"

"Grandpa's fine. He's taking a long-wished-for summer with his sister in Wisconsin."

Cyndi grinned at them, adding, "And I've begun working in the fire tower at the far edge of his farmland."

"You are there alone?" Carlita asked, and when Cyndi nodded, she added, "You must come home to dinner with us."

"Please," she entreated when Cyndi hesitated. "That is, if you haven't something else planned."

"No. My day is free," Cyndi responded. "But I don't want to be a bother. You weren't expecting me."

"That's no problem," Al chuckled. "Carlita always seems able to stretch a meal; something *Abuelita* taught her."

"*Abuelita* means grandmother in Spanish," Carlita explained. "Our parents passed away before we were married; they died quite young. So when we decided to move to Indiana, we brought Grandma with us."

Cyndi drove behind the Hernandez station wagon in her car to their home on the other side of the small town. It was one of the rambling, homey places that had been there on the oak-tree lined street almost since the town began.

They followed little Luz as she scampered across the well-kept lawn and up the steps onto a wide veranda.

"Welcome to our home, Cynthia," Al stated warmly, opening the door into a pleasant living room.

"Take her to meet Grandmother while I finish getting dinner ready," Carlita said, taking Luz's hand and heading down a long hall.

"Come," Al invited Cyndi, smiling as he walked across the living room and a few steps down another, shorter hall to the door of what appeared to be a combination bedroom/sitting room.

Sunshine filtered brightly through white lace curtains onto the top of a small, well-polished desk and the muted pastel colors of a patchwork quilt folded on a long, low trunk at the end of the bed.

Cyndi's gaze continued over the lovely handmade lace spread and flower-embroidered pillows to the other side of the room. Then she saw her, almost a part of the pleasant setting itself.

"Abuelita Evetia, may we come in?" Al asked softly. "I want you to meet Cynthia Carlson," he added, crossing the room to another sun-brightened window where a petite, white-haired lady in a blue dress sat in a small upholstered rocker. Sparkling black eyes turned their gaze to Cyndi, a welcoming smile brightening the face of Al's grandmother.

"Carlson?" her crocheted shawl slipped from her shoulder as she held her slim brown hand out to Cyndi. "Is she David's little girl, Alfredito?"

"She's his granddaughter, Abuelita."

"Ah, yes. I sometimes forget the quick passing of the years." She laughed softly at herself as she clasped Cyndi's hand. "You are very pretty, my dear."

"Thank you." Cyndi smiled a bit self-consciously.

"Alfredito, please pull that stool over here for her so we may get acquainted. You do not mind, Cynthia?"

"That would be nice," Cyndi answered. "Unless Carlita needs me to help her."

"I'll help if she does," Al said, placing a short, cushioned stool near the rocker.

Evetia closed the Bible lying in her lap, placing the book and her reading glasses on the wide windowsill next to a potted geranium.

"This is a day when arthritis plagues me heavily, making it almost impossible to walk, so I stayed home from church services," Evetia explained, shifting a bit in her rocker, holding tightly to its polished arms as she did so.

"Alfredito, dear boy, wanted to carry me to the car, but I told him no. I would worship my Lord here today. This rocker is a special place, anyway, where I spend much time talking with the Lord and reading His Word."

Evetia reached out to place her hand on Cyndi's soft curls. "Do you know the One about whom I speak?"

Cyndi nodded, her eyes misting as she remembered her recent neglect.

"Long ago, when I was a little girl living near Cheran," Evetia said, "our priest was a close friend of my family and spent many hours talking with me and my brothers about the Savior as we walked into the foothills to gather firewood for my mother."

"Where is Cheran?" Cyndi asked.

"It is in the state of Michcacan in west-central Mexico. A lovely place of many trees where we had fields filled with flowers of a variety of colors. We had no snow, but it sometimes got very cold. There were rabbits and squirrels and many birds."

"Do you get lonesome for Cheran?" Cyndi asked.

"Sometimes," Evetia answered, a faraway look in her eyes. "Sometimes I get lonesome to see the adobe walls and red-tile roofs of Cheran, but my family is here, so this is where I belong now. And I have been an American citizen for many years, but we keep my ancestry alive with some of the old family names.

"And your family, Cynthia," she continued. "Besides your grandfather, where are they?"

"My brother, David, is in Illinois training in a Bible school. Our parents are in Mexico for a while, but farther south than your Cheran. They're in the Yukatan, assisting Rev. Barlow and Father Kiepura who are working together in a very poor area. They give work and financial assistance to the people there while at the same time sharing the gospel with them."

"That is good," Evetia said. "We also were extremely poor in Cheran; it was difficult for the families. There was a great lack of employment opportunities, and those available paid very meager wages. It was a struggle always," Evetia sighed.

"The fathers and boys cultivated corn and beans, squash and mustard, but often the weather was against them and we had even less those years. Here it has not been so, except in the beginning when my husband first brought me to the States. Always there has been enough to eat."

"Dinner, Abuelita, dinner!" little Luz cried, dashing into the room to lean against her great-grandmother's knee. "Daddy carry you; he's coming."

Later in the afternoon as Carlita walked with Cyndi to her car, she said, "It was so nice having you here. Will you come again? And give your grandfather our regards. We miss him."

"Yes, thank you," Cyndi answered. "And I know Grandpa will be glad to hear from you. I expect to write to him in the next few days unless he gives me a call first."

As she drove home, Cyndi wondered how Tim was feeling but decided not to phone, afraid she might disturb him or his father who Grandpa had said was injured.

The next morning she went earlier than usual to the tower, wanting to watch the sunrise from that vantage point.

Swinging one of the windows open, she pulled the tall chair over and sat down, resting her arm on the sill.

The air was very cool and moist against her skin; aromas of the forest drifted up, pleasantly reminding her of moss and bark.

As Cyndi watched, the forest seemed to gradually fill with soft green light. She was deeply stirred by the beauty and solitude of this place.

Streaks of color began to tinge the sky with such beauty that Cyndi felt she could never express the enormity of its glory as it spread from horizon to horizon in bands of flourescent hues. She wished she had colored pencils or chalks along to at least get a sketch of color placements.

When the sun burst forth over the sea of treetops, fluttering leaves of white-trunked aspen twinkled like a shimmering stream among the miles of green. Cyndi drew in her breath.

"Thank you for my eyesight, Lord," she whispered. "I will never forget this moment, this incredible sight."

Late that afternoon, glancing up from her textbook, she saw that a storm was forming in the distance toward the west. She watched in amazement as lightning flashed in that area amid dark cloud masses, while off to the east, that entire expanse was basking in sunshine.

I love this place, she thought. *I almost feel as though I could spend the rest of my life here.*

She reflected seriously on that for a moment, knowing she could never make a living by manning a fire tower—at least not the type of life she had been planning for years.

Cyndi pushed that line of thought away and turned back to her book and note pad.

Tim phoned that evening shortly after her supper. "I'm afraid I slept a good part of yesterday away," he told her. "To-day, except for some time in the tower, I've been trying to catch up on some work for Dad. How are things going for you?"

"Just fine, Tim. You had a nice day for outdoor work."

"Sure did. Hope it stays this way all week. I'll be away on weekends for a month or so and probably won't get to see you. I'll try to catch you on the phone or radio at the tower a few times during the week. Can we have dinner together this Thursday night?"

"I'd like that. Who's cooking? Or should we have another picnic?"

"Wrong on both counts," Tim chuckled. "For once I'm taking you to a restaurant. It's just a small one in town, but their fried chicken and catfish are delicious. Eight o'clock okay?"

"Sounds good. See you then."

Cyndi left the tower an hour early Thursday so she would have time to wash and dry her hair. She dressed carefully, an-ticipating her date with Tim.

She put on a stylish beige dress that had speckles of bur-gundy flowers on it. She slipped into tan pumps, put a small spray of perfume on, and was locking the front door behind her when Tim's van rolled up the graveled drive.

He jumped out and had her door open by the time she reached him.

"I hear something that sounds like sleighbells," she men-tioned, standing by the car, listening.

"It's the spring-peepers singing," Tim answered.

"They're tiny black frogs that sing in the springtime. I hadn't thought of them sounding like sleighbells before but that's pretty accurate."

Then, bending low in an exaggerated bow and with a sweep of his hand, he intoned, "Enter my chariot, Princess; the steeds await."

Cyndi giggled. "I thought it was too early in the year for pumpkins, O Prince."

Backing the van to the road, Tim grinned appreciatively at her. "You sure are a pretty picture."

"I'm glad you think so," Cyndi responded.

The restaurant was small but pleasant with armchairs at the round tables and framed flower-prints on the cream-colored walls.

Squat candles in milk-glass holders with bouquets of wildflowers centered on the white tablecloths were an attractive touch.

"This is nice, Tim," Cyndi said, settling into the comfortable chair.

Tim nodded, and began to look over the menu.

"I'll miss you the next few weeks," Cyndi admitted later as they lingered over dessert. "You'll be so busy, and away on the weekends."

"That works both ways," Tim smiled. "We do have fun together, don't we? When I'm back and we have an afternoon free, I want to take you on a special ride."

"Where?"

"Sorry, I can't tell you; it's a surprise." Tim's blue eyes sparkled with mischief. "But I will tell you that you're probably not used to this kind of transportation."

Cyndi thought about it occasionally over the next month, trying to guess where Tim planned to take her. But other things were happening to keep her mind busy.

It was a quiet, misty evening following an afternoon of sporadic light showers. Cyndi was sitting at the kitchen table trying to concentrate on Advanced Business Administration when the phone rang sharply in the stillness.

"Cynthia, this is Carlita Hernandez. Would you be free to spend tomorrow with me?"

"Sure. What do you have in mind?"

"A short hike in the morning, then some shopping, and later supper with my family," Carlita answered.

"That sounds great. I can be ready anytime after about seven a.m."

"Come over then; that time is perfect."

"Okay; bye." Cyndi hung up the receiver, looking forward to the next day.

Because shopping and being a supper guest were to be part of her day following the hike, Cyndi decided against jeans the next morning and instead dressed in casual tan pants and white shirt and carried a light jacket for the possibly cool evening.

She clasped a thin silver chain around her neck and went to the kitchen for the small basket of eggs she had gotten ready as a gift.

Appreciation was evident on Carlita's face as she opened the door to Cyndi's knock. Leading the way into the kitchen, she transferred the eggs from the basket to a bowl in the refrigerator.

"How about a cup of coffee, Cynthia?" she offered.

"Great, and please call me Cyndi," she said, seating herself at the table. "Where are we hiking to?"

"Not far; down a back road to the forest's edge," Carlita answered, lining Cyndi's egg basket with paper towels.

"Here." Carlita handed her the basket, saying, "Do you mind carrying this along?"

"I don't mind." Cyndi smiled at her, feeling a sense of

friendship developing with this woman who was about ten years older than she.

Carlita's long, dark hair glistened in the sunshine in pretty contrast to Cyndi's blond curls as they crossed the backyard. They passed a small vegetable garden where newly set tomato plants soaked up the sun behind rows of cabbage and brussels sprouts, and other plants Cyndi didn't recognize.

"Even with all these salad makings"—Carlita gestured toward a plot of young onions, radishes, and masses of red and green lettuces—"Grandma still likes to have wild greens occasionally. And I must admit, I enjoy them, too."

Cyndi smiled at her questioningly. "That's where we're going? To pick a salad?"

"Yes. We'll get the main items from the garden later along with some tender young dandelion greens from the yard, but we'll be able to find nice mustards and chick-weed and wild sorrel."

"I've never gathered a salad this way," Cyndi admitted. "Although I've read about people doing this."

"The important thing is to not pick from plants along a well-traveled road," Carlita advised, "because there can be toxic residues on the plants from vehicle exhausts. But we needn't worry about that too much around here."

Carlita opened a gate at the back of the garden to a path leading through an oak-studded field of grass. "My brother kept his horse in here while he was still at home with us. He lives in the northern part of the state now."

Later, when they were heading back to Carlita's house, she said, "When I have extra time, I often go to the stream near the old gristmill for watercress, but that's too far for today."

"Have you always known about these items being available for food?"Cyndi asked.

"Yes. My parents were quite poor when I was a child, but

we always managed to have a large garden. They also taught us that God had provided many free foods if we would take time to look for them."

After picking what they wanted from the yard and garden, they stopped at a bed of pansies where Carlita picked several of the flower heads, white, violet and yellow, laying them on top of the basket of greens and small vegetables.

"Those aren't edible, are they?" Cyndi exclaimed.

"Yes, surprisingly, they are," Carlita answered. "And they make such beautiful garnishes. Violets and primroses do too. Grandma Evetia likes to use them, especially when she makes salad for guests."

A boy who appeared to Cyndi to be about thirteen was in the kitchen when they returned, standing by a counter near the door.

"Cyndi, this is my son, Juan," Carlita stated.

The two smiled at each other, acknowledging the introduction. Little Luz grinned from her tall stool at the table where she sat spooning cereal into her mouth next to Evetia.

Cyndi walked over to greet Evetia, and Carlita said, "You didn't have to help with the early preparations for tonight's dinner, Grandma."

"I know, but Juan helped me get out here and then fixed breakfast for the three of us, so I got started on making some tiny tortillas. With a bit of meat and salsa, they'll be fine appetizers before your baked chicken."

"Thanks, Grandma." Carlita gave her a hug. "We'll all appreciate that nice addition."

Carlita turned to Cyndi, saying, "I'm glad you could be here while our Juan is home. He was spending the weekend with a new friend when you were with us before."

Juan grinned at his mother. "I hadn't told you earlier because I wanted to be sure, but Dan said he can get me a job on his dad's farm as soon as school's out next week. Won't that be great?"

"Yes, it will," she agreed heartily. To Cyndi she explained, "Mr. Zodest is new at the bank in town, but he also has rented a vacant farm, from what Dan told Juan, and will have an out-of-town relative of his work it this summer."

"I feel real lucky," Juan declared. "It's sometimes hard for a kid my age to find a job paying much."

"Yes, I can understand that." Cyndi smiled at him as she picked up a dish towel to dry the dishes he was washing. "My brother, David, and I often had that same problem."

Cyndi felt a comfortable sense of companionship in the homey kitchen working beside the young boy who, like David, didn't seem to feel it degrading to help in the kitchen.

"Look." Juan lifted a soapy hand to point out the window over the sink. A bluejay perched with its fluffy baby on a branch of a tree where honeybees reveled in the nectar of large yellow-green flowers.

Early that evening while finishing touches were being put on the dinner table and Juan was helping Luz fasten the back of her dress, the doorbell rang.

"Cyndi, will you please get the door?" Carlita called from the kitchen. "Al must have misplaced his key."

But it wasn't Al on the porch.

Cyndi glanced out the front window and caught a glimpse of the back of a shiny white car.

She opened the door to find herself confronted by two police officers—the same pair she had observed snooping around Grandpa's farm.

Before she realized who they were, the darker of the two men, without waiting for an invitation, pushed the door open wider and stepped inside.

4

The blond young man followed the other one inside, but the first one stopped suddenly, seemingly as surprised as Cyndi. Then Luz ran into the room and straight into his arms.

"We're here, sis," he called, seeing Carlita leaving the kitchen and coming through the hall to see what the commotion was about.

"Oh, I'm so glad you could make it!" she exclaimed. "But you had said you would have to be late, if you got away at all.

"Cyndi," she continued, "this is my brother, Lucio Gembe."

"And this is my friend, Jeff Thornburg, Carlita; Cyndi."

"We're happy to have you with us, Jeff." Carlita shook his hand. "Lucio said he hoped you would be free this evening."

Juan joined them in the living room after the two young men had greeted Evetia, and Cyndi had an opportunity to get acquainted with Lucio and Jeff before all were called to supper.

A week later, after a day of rain showers and tiring study, Cyndi was feeling fatigued and a little lonely when the phone rang.

"Cyndi, this is Jeff Thornburg. We met at the Hernandez home last Saturday."

"Yes, Jeff. It was a nice evening, wasn't it?"

"Sure was. I realize this is very short notice, but Lucio wants me to join him for a double date at a concert in the city tomorrow, and you're the only girl I'm acquainted with in this area." He chuckled. "That didn't come out right, did it? I'd consider it an honor if you would go with us. How about it?"

"I'd enjoy that very much, Jeff," she answered sincerely, "even if you are caught dateless at the last minute and I'm your only possibility." Cyndi laughed lightly.

"We want to have dinner there before the concert, so we'll have to leave early because of the long drive," he added. "Will you be able to leave around three in the afternoon?"

"That'll be fine, Jeff. See you." Cyndi's fatigue seemed to lift as she replaced the receiver. How nice it would be to get to know her new friends better, to dress up and hear some good music.

She was glad she had brought along at least one special outfit even though she hadn't really expected to need it. Remembering her mother's admonition made her smile. *"Always be prepared for any eventuality if you possibly can."*

She missed David and her parents, especially her mom and the good talks they had together. They were the best of friends as well as mother and daughter, for which Cyndi was both thankful and proud when she had heard comments from some of her friends about their family relationships.

Cyndi sighed. She knew her mom had been disappointed at her goal of financial independence. She could have caused conflict by trying to discourage Cyndi. Instead, she had stressed God's priorities that *she* had learned through difficult times of thinking material things had more importance than they really did.

Because she had known Mom's words were true, the struggle in her heart had been intensifying lately.

These thoughts were in her mind throughout the next day even when she was studying her college work, and she found herself sending up short, silent prayers for direction.

Cyndi felt happy and rather elegant that afternoon as Jeff escorted her in her plain, black dress to the backseat of a refurbished yellow convertible.

She settled down beside the attractive redhead introduced as Jennifer Martin. Jennifer was dressed in a green dress that set off her creamy, freckle-sprinkled complexion.

"We thought sitting together on the drive there would give you girls a chance to get acquainted," Jeff said.

"And we're leaving the top up," Lucio said from behind the wheel, "so the wind doesn't mess up your pretty hair."

Cyndi learned that Jennifer and Lucio were childhood friends and were very fond of each other; her appreciation for the other girl grew throughout the drive, and by the time they reached the restaurant they felt like old friends.

The sun was low on the horizon when they entered the city and parked by the marble-and-glass front of the restaurant.

Soft music from a trio of violinists set the mood in the large, carpeted room where the four were escorted beneath shimmering chandeliers to a table set with cut crystal and a linen tablecloth.

Ah, this is my kind of living, Cyndi thought, as she slipped her sweater from her shoulders onto the soft velvet upholstery of the high-backed chair.

She glanced casually around the grandly appointed room at the expensively dressed diners seated at the other tables. Strategically placed potted palms and beautiful urns of cut flowers formed an oasis of partial privacy for each table.

Following a delicate soup, they were served crisp salads set off with intricately cut garnishes. Cyndi's thoughts turned to wild salads with flower blossoms, all gathered at no cost, given freely by God.

Although she felt sure that the majority of Christians indulged in costly meals at least occasionally, she felt a slight uneasiness because of her delight in these lavish surroundings, the almost ostentatious service of the well-tailored waiters as they brought the entrees on fine china and silver platters.

Am I truly going to be able to accept whatever God has planned for me to do with my life if it means having less financially than I've been counting on?

Cyndi pushed the thought aside, deciding not to let it intrude and spoil her evening. *After all, what can be wrong with enjoying the finer things of the world? If I'm trying to live right by not giving in to sin, don't I deserve some of the extra luxuries of life?*

Even as her thoughts persisted in arguing back and forth, she knew deep down that she was just trying to excuse her greed.

As though reading her thoughts, Lucio said with a grin, "Jeff is used to this style as daily fare, but it is the first time Jennifer has received the royal treatment from me. Frankly, I wouldn't be able to afford it very often, but I'm splurging tonight because the occasion is one of the most important in my life. It's extremely special."

He reached over to Jennifer, putting his hand on the sheer sleeve of her dress and his eyes held a gentle look as he said, "I planned to announce our engagement tonight, which is why I wanted my best friend, Jeff, here. Jennifer has promised to become my wife sometime during the next year."

"Congratulations!" Jeff raised his water goblet as though making a toast. "I suspected this would be happening soon. Lucio spends half his time talking about you, Jen," he added, smiling at her, obviously happy for them.

"Abuelita already knows," Lucio said, "but we wanted to surprise the rest of the family. We'll tell them tomorrow."

Later, after the uplifting concert, as they were fastening their seat belts for the drive back to Milltown, Jeff said, "It makes an old bachelor's heart rejoice to see two fine people decide to join their lives."

"Yes," Cyndi agreed, "but you're not much older than Lucio, are you?"

"Only a few years, actually. I'm twenty-seven, but when a fellow hasn't found his one-and-only girl by then, it's easy at times like this to be aware of the passing years."

"Well, even thirty is still quite young," Cyndi remarked, wondering what it would be like to be the "one-and-only" girl of a man like Jeff.

He seems very pleasant and considerate, and from what Lucio said, must be well-off financially.

Lucio had lowered the convertible's top, allowing the glorious panorama of the nighttime sky above them to be seen in its full beauty. The air was brisk but not too cool as it rushed over them, and traffic was light, making driving pleasant.

Lucio began singing with a fine tenor voice. Cyndi felt sure it was a Spanish love song, although she didn't recognize the melody.

"Lucio told me his grandmother taught him many songs in her original language," Jeff said. "He enjoys singing them and keeps in practice partly for her sake, too, I think. They seem to be a close-knit family—each one so loving and concerned about the others."

"I've noticed that too," Cyndi agreed. "It reminds me of my own family."

Lucio's song ended and Cyndi rested her head against the back of the seat so she could better see the beauty of the sky.

"Look at the Milky Way and the Big Dipper! Aren't they spectacular tonight!" she exclaimed.

Jeff didn't answer for a moment, then very slowly he quoted against the rushing wind:

The heavens declare the glory of God;
And the firmament showeth His handiwork . . .

There is no speech or language where their voice is not heard.
Their line is gone out through all the earth,
And their words to the end of the world.

"That's from somewhere in the Psalms, isn't it?" Cynthia asked.

"Yes," he answered. "I'm a Christian and God's Word is very important to me."

"Jeff, I'm a Christian, too."

"I thought so," he said, gently touching her hand.

Cyndi thought, *He's got that going for him, too—he's a Christian.*

Then her thoughts drifted to Tim—the tall, lanky frame, the gentle blue eyes, and fun personality. *Is he a Christian?* she wondered. *He never mentioned it, although he did quote that scripture from Isaiah. Mom always stressed the importance of not caring for someone who doesn't know the Lord, but that's exactly what I did with Mark. Nice as he was, he didn't attend church or express any interest at all in that direction.*

Gazing at the majesty of the stars, she asked, "Why did you become a policeman, Jeff? Is someone in your family an officer?"

"No, my family's business is a large brokerage firm which I was expected to enter. It's always been run with integrity, but I didn't feel it was what I was supposed to do with my life—at least not for now."

Jeff clasped his hands behind his head, deep in thought. In the light from a passing car, Cyndi could see the finely chiseled outline of his profile, a refined handsomeness beneath the thick blond hair blowing back from his forehead.

Jeff continued. "I know it doesn't happen often, and that the percentage is small, but I had read several times of police officers who didn't do their duty, who were lax or corrupt in some way, and it bothered me a lot.

"I felt drawn to the profession and decided to be the very best officer I could, someone kids could look up to, a man people could sincerely respect."

"Is the job what you expected?" Cyndi asked.

"Yes and no. I enjoy the work even more than I thought I would, but I can understand the lure of wrongdoing or looking the other way that some officers give in to. There are many opportunities, even pressures, for doing the wrong thing, but it doesn't have to happen—the giving in to them, I mean. It's the same in other areas of life."

Cyndi smiled to herself, recalling her sense of dread or fear the day she had first seen Jeff and Lucio on the road at the edge of Grandpa's farm. Certainly, there could be nothing to distrust in these two. Yet she did wonder about what she had considered strange actions at the time—unless they had been hunting a fugitive. But she had heard nothing on the news about that.

Cyndi wasn't sure whether she should pry into his work, so instead she asked, "Do you come to this area often, Jeff? Carlita said Lucio was stationed in the northern part of the state."

Jeff hesitated a moment before answering. "Lucio invited me along when he came for a visit last weekend. It was nice to meet his family and a welcome change from my usual routine."

Last weekend? Cyndi's thoughts were confused. *I wonder why he didn't mention the earlier time. I'm sure it was them I saw near Grandpa's about two weeks ago . . .* She knew she wouldn't want to admit that she had been fearful just because they were policemen, so she steered the conversation to other topics.

Because it was so late when they arrived back in the Milltown area, the three didn't accept Cyndi's offer of a cup of coffee before they went on.

"I think I'll be back in this area next weekend, Cyndi," Jeff ventured. "Any chance I can spend some time with you again? Friday evening, maybe, for dinner and a drive? Lucio and Jennifer would be our guests."

"I'd like that," Cyndi said, "if seven o'clock is okay. I usually stay in the tower until six unless it's raining."

"Sounds fine. Incidentally, if you always leave the tower at six, who reports fires that start during the night?"

"Few fires break out at night," Cyndi explained, "because the wind usually dies down by six unless it's stormy."

Because of that fact, she couldn't understand the bright flashes she observed a few nights later at about eight o'clock.

The day had been exceptionally hot for so early in the season, so she stayed overtime in the tower, feeling it would be cooler at that height once the sun had set. She read until well after sundown, then sat watching the twilight settle over the landscape of treetops below as she silently talked to the Lord about the questions and conflict that had been bothering her lately.

Cyndi watched the flashes intently for a while before determining that instead of distant bits of flame, they appeared to be lights of some sort and much closer than she had at first thought. Dismissing them, since they posed no danger to the forest, she went to where the radio rested on top of its iron box and prepared to lock it inside for the night.

It was then a voice from the radio broke the evening stillness, a man's voice she didn't recognize as any she occasionally heard from conversations of passing truckers on surrounding highways.

"This location seems okay, Joe. How about yours?"

"Told you not to use my name," another voice answered. "We'll discuss the locations next time we meet."

"Okay, J—. Sorry, I mean forty-seven."

Cyndi listened a few minutes more, but there was only silence so she locked the radio in the iron box, wondering why the men were acting so secretive. Were they involved in some sort of crime, she wondered, or were they just playing a game of some type?

The moon had risen over the distant hills by the time she left the tower, giving enough light so she didn't have to grope her way down the flights of stairs in the dusk as she had thought she might.

Out of curiosity, Cyndi stayed late in the tower Thursday too. As twilight fell, she scanned the general area where she thought the lights had been but saw only the darker shadows of the forest. *It was evidently nothing important*, she decided.

But as she picked up her tote and bent to lift the trapdoor, her gaze crossed to the window at one side of the room and she saw the flickering lights again. Only they weren't in the same location as the previous night. This time they seemed to be a mile or so to the west.

Her interest heightened now, she got out her binoculars and peered carefully at the area. They were definitely lights of some sort, but she couldn't imagine what kind or why they would be in a secluded area of the forest. From what she recalled from the map, there weren't any roads nearby, except for a narrow one used occasionally by park-service trucks. She could think of no reason for anyone to be there this late. If that weren't such an isolated area, she would have thought some campers had lost their way on a nighttime hike.

Suddenly the radio crackled to life. "Calling twenty-seven; calling twenty-seven. Hurry up, for Pete's sake!"

"This is twenty-seven. What'd ya want?"

"Want you to flash section one at nine Monday."

"Morning or night?"

"Night, of course; just as usual!"

"Section one, nine Monday. Gotcha, forty-seven."

"Forty-seven! Of course!" Cyndi remembered. "The voices I overheard a few nights ago."

The radio crackled a moment, then the first voice, now

identified as forty-seven, said roughly, "And don't mess up like in Illinois!"

"Ya, ya, I know. So I made a little mistake. So kill me."

Cyndi had the disturbing feeling that what was going on between those two was definitely not a simple game. She wondered if she should mention it to someone, but even if there was mischief going on, what could anyone do about a couple of random voices that could have originated from anywhere in a fairly large area?

Cyndi decided to ask Tim when she was with him again. She missed him and would be glad when the next two weeks had passed. Too, she was curious about the unusual ride he had promised to give her. It sounded intriguing, and she was looking forward to it.

For now, though, she thought, *Jeff is coming tomorrow night with Lucio and Jennifer. I liked being with her, too. I think she'll be a good friend.*

Friday evening Cyndi put on the same dress she had worn the week before on her date with Jeff. But instead of the gold necklace and earrings, she clasped a single strand of pearls around her neck and wore pearl earrings.

Stepping into the low pumps that matched her dress, she settled her light cardigan sweater over her shoulders.

When Jeff knocked on the front door, she put the matter out of her thoughts.

Cyndi enjoyed being with the three of them even more than she had the previous time.

Lucio drove Jennifer's car again, one she said had been her brother's before he moved away to a more lucrative position and bought a new one.

Following a delicious dinner in a larger town not far away, they went for a drive through some of the more scenic spots in the nearby areas.

"How beautiful!" Cyndi exclaimed when they stopped at the top of a bluff in a pull-off area to view the vista below. Stars were emerging in a sky still faintly streaked with pink and gold at the horizon.

Below was a panorama of faintly discernible forest interspersed with blocks of farmland and clusters of lights from widely spaced small towns.

Car lights like a moving string of diamonds flowed along intersecting highways, but it was quiet with no sound of vehicles reaching the high bluff. The four young people got out of the car and stood at the edge of the gravel area watching as twilight turned to dark.

"I have a blanket in the car," Jennifer said. "If everyone would like to, we could spread it on the long bench over there and talk awhile."

"Good idea," Lucio agreed as he headed back to get the blanket.

After they had settled themselves comfortably, Jeff turned sideways so he was partly facing the others, his arm along the backrest behind Cyndi. "It's hard to realize the tragedy those miles of highway may contain before the night is over, considering how serene they look from up here."

"You're thinking about what we were discussing earlier?" Lucio asked.

"Yes."

"What's that?" Jennifer questioned.

"Several things," Lucio began, "but we were talking mainly about narcotics, specifically marijuana."

Cyndi shuddered. "David, my brother, warned me about marijuana when I was quite young, because some of the kids at his school smoked it. Fortunately, he had paid attention to warnings about the danger of experimenting with it."

"He was smart." Jeff said. "Lots of guys get fooled, girls too—pulled into it by a friend who tells them it can't hurt them."

"It's smoked like a regular cigarette, isn't it?" Jennifer asked.

"Yes," Lucio answered, "although it can be used in other ways and often is, some of them quite insidious."

"One of the subtle dangers is that people are told it's non-addictive, that nothing can happen to them other than 'getting high,' " Jeff said, warming to the subject. "But that's not true. There are many hazards, mainly the long-term effects of the THC."

"What's that?" Cyndi asked.

"It's the psychoactive chemical in marijuana that can change a person's behavior and thought pattern, in addition to the effects that show up in almost every system of the body," he answered.

"You both sound so serious about it."

"We *are* serious," Lucio looked earnestly at Cyndi. "Dead serious, because there's a frightening increase in the number of deaths among young people who are getting involved in this and other drug use."

"It actually kills them?" Cyndi exclaimed.

"Sometimes, over long term," he answered. "But often quicker, indirectly, through accidents and murder—even suicide."

"How terrible!" Cyndi and Jennifer said almost in unison.

Jennifer leaned forward. "Aren't people aware of the price they may be paying when they start using drugs?"

"They obviously don't believe the warnings they do hear," Lucio explained—"or the urgings of their friends are more important."

"That's so sad," Cyndi said, gazing at the view without seeing it.

"Yes," Jeff agreed, "it is. It causes a lot of grief and heartache. That's why we try so hard to spread information about it to the schools, and to—"

"And?" Jennifer asked.

Jeff hesitated and Lucio said, "Keep away from any aspect of it, because one problem of great concern is the fact that the potency of the product has increased in recent years in spot samples from street vendors. It's use can cause a lot of damage because the potency of any one joint can't be judged just by looking at—"

"It's all so depressing!" Jennifer broke in. "Can't we just put the problem aside for now and enjoy the evening?"

"Sorry, Jen," he apologized. "Guess we were acting as if we were giving a lecture." He put his arm around her shoulders and pointed upward. "See that formation of stars there, beyond those three? Isn't it beautiful?"

The following Sunday, Cyndi decided to visit the old mill. After the church service, she packed a lunch and drove to the spot where she and Tim had shared a picnic. She wished he was along now. He had phoned Friday morning to remind her of the ride they would be taking the next weekend.

"I've been trying to guess where you're going to take me," she had pried.

"You'll see some great sights," he had answered, giving her no clues.

Now she spread her blanket under the trees and relaxed, eating her sandwiches and enjoying the peaceful afternoon.

While she thought about her friendships with Tim and Jeff, the similarities and differences in the two men, she watched a little screech owl drowsing on a limb high above her and marveled at an industrious pair of chickadees enlarging an old woodpecker feeding hole, making it adequate for the small nest she supposed they would build there.

After a while she got up, locked her picnic things in the car, and headed down the remembered path to the mill, cool beneath the canopy of leaves.

The path led through open areas, where red paintbrush and white Queen Anne's lace were coming into bloom and down past a grove of spruce before she came to the rushing narrow stream.

Cyndi noticed the cattails had grown taller in the quiet edge of the water, and large clumps of tawny orange day lilies were beginning to brighten the area with their beauty.

"I can understand why Tim thought this would make a pretty setting for a home," she mused. "The old stone mill has a great quality of strength and timelessness about it, even though it's run down now." She wondered if the miller and his family had lived in the mill itself or had a house nearby.

She decided to hike into the forest around the area someday soon and see if she could find evidence of any other buildings. There was something about relics from the past that always fascinated her.

She was picking a few of the day lilies for a kitchen-table bouquet when she noticed at the edge of the stream the patch of watercress Carlita had mentioned.

Being careful not to slip on the wet rocks, she gathered several handfuls of the pungent green. She was making her way back to the shore when she saw the paper.

It was partly wadded and caught in an eddy where shallower water flowed over some small rocks among the cattails at the edge of the stream. Because litter disfiguring the landscape annoyed her, she reached out among the stems to get the paper, intending to put it in the trash container at home.

As she walked back along the path, she tried to uncrumple the paper and shake the water off before she got it to the car.

Startled, she suddenly stood still, staring at the wet, wrinkled sheet in her hand. It was half a torn sheet, jagged along the top edge, but she recognized it anyway because of her work in the tower.

It was part of a map, an enlargement of a portion of the

state forest—a part very familiar to her, the area containing Redbud fire tower, her tower.

A red pencil mark circled two small sections of land to the north of the tower, one a bit west of the other.

Cyndi's curiosity quickly turned to alarm because of the red X that covered the tower location. Her alarm rapidly evolved into a sense of fear that crawled up her spine when her gaze caught the notation in the bottom right-hand corner of the map: "For twenty-seven."

5

Twenty-seven, one of the voices on the radio!

Cyndi hurried the rest of the way to her car and drove home, feeling afraid of some unknown danger.

Be sensible, she chided herself, smoothing the piece of map on the kitchen table. *There must be some logical explanation.* But the vague feeling of apprehension stayed with her through the night and the first part of the next day.

Tim phoned her at the tower around eleven Monday morning to ask if he could stop by at noon and take her out to lunch.

"I've already got my lunch up here with me," she told him.

"Bring it along," he chuckled.

Cyndi was sitting on the tower's bottom step with her lunch in her tote when Tim arrived in his yellow van.

"Hi," he grinned as she got in. "As long as you had already prepared a sack lunch, I decided to make one, too. I'll take you to an unusual picnic spot."

They chatted comfortably, happy to be together again as Tim drove what seemed to Cyndi about twenty-five miles. He finally turned onto a small gravel road and pulled in beneath a clump of white-trunked birch trees. Not far away was a long, low building and beyond it a wide, open field.

Cyndi looked questioningly at Tim, but he just grinned, saying nothing and opening the brown bag beside him, handing her a container of crisp radishes and celery sticks, then unwrapping a sandwich.

Cyndi was finishing the first half of her egg-salad sandwich when a small red plane taxied from behind the building, made a turn, and picked up speed as it crossed the open expanse, taking off, rising to the east.

"So this is an airport," she said. "I wasn't aware there was one here."

"There was no reason you should have known," Tim stated. "It's located just beyond the edge of the map your Alidade covers."

"So that's our special ride. You're going to take me up in a plane."

"Not exactly," Tim teased.

"Not exactly? It's got to be either yes or no."

"Actually, it's yes and no," he answered, grinning.

"You're exasperating, Tim Nichols." She was unable to keep from smiling herself. "It can't be both."

"But it is." Unwrapping another sandwich he continued, "I'll show you as soon as we've finished eating."

After they had shared her cookies and finished his thermos of lemonade, they got out of the van. Tim held out his hand, taking hers as he led her to the long white aluminum-covered building.

As they walked past the end of the structure, Tim waved through a window at a middle-aged man bending over a desk. When they rounded the corner, Cyndi saw that there were several planes inside the hangar portion of the building and a small helicopter outside at the far end.

"Browse around for a few minutes if you want to," Tim suggested. "I've got to go in and sign the log."

Cyndi walked the length of the hangar, glancing in at the planes, exchanging a wave with a mechanic working on one of them. Then she moved around the forest-green helicopter, wondering how anyone could feel safe in a plastic bubble that looked only large enough for two people to fit comfortably.

"Ready to climb in?"

Cyndi jumped, startled because she hadn't heard Tim walk up behind her on the concrete.

"Hardly," she said with a little laugh. "There doesn't seem to be enough there to keep it aloft. Afraid I'd be scared to death. Which one are we going in—really?"

"This is it, Cyndi," he stated, putting a key in the lock opening the see-through door.

"I don't know, Tim. This looks pretty scary." She felt a little embarrassed at her hesitation.

"A girl who likes tower work will certainly enjoy this." He took her elbow to assist her up into the cabin, giving her no time to back down.

Cyndi settled down into the comfortable seat and carefully buckled up the safety belt. Tim slipped into the seat beside her, fastened his belt, and started the engine.

She heard the chop-chop-chop of the rotors on top of the helicopter beginning to turn. Then the chopping sound became more intense as the whirling blades picked up speed.

The engine roared and she felt the motor's power as the ship began to vibrate. Tim lifted easily on a lever that extended from behind the left side of his seat, and they rose as if by magic to several feet above the ground.

Cyndi was enjoying the floating sensation, but intrigued by what Tim was doing, she watched him closely. As he raised the lever, he also pressed on a stick rising from the floor between his knees, and they moved forward a bit.

"Okay?" he asked.

"Let's go," Cyndi answered, not feeling all that ready for it.

Tim pushed forward on the stick again and the little aircraft pushed forward into the wind. Then he gave a little back pressure on the control and they started climbing and moving forward. The ascent increased sharply. Cyndi drew in her breath while they cleared the hangar not many feet away by a wide margin.

"Well?" Tim asked, smiling broadly.

"What a thrill; you had me off guard there," Cyndi laughed, looking down through the transparent plastic surrounding them to the airport not far below. She saw Tim pull back on the stick and simultaneously push down on the lever. Suddenly they were just hovering above and to one side of the clump of birch and trees and the van.

"Was it difficult learning to fly this?" Cyndi questioned.

"No. It's different from a plane but not harder, necessarily," Tim answered.

"Grandpa mentioned that you already had a pilot's license," Cyndi added.

"That's right. I'd also had extra training in pilot's weather, so the only thing needed was helicopter school, which I finished last summer. That's what I've been doing the past weekends, too—continuing my training by learning the mechanics of the machine so I can repair it when necessary. I wanted some more flight time before I took you up with me, so I got some of that in, too, while I was away."

"You've certainly been busy." Cyndi was thoroughly impressed.

"Sure have, but I enjoyed every minute of it. When I can get a free block of time, I'd like to go to Texas for an intensive course in whirlybird mechanics," Tim continued.

"Seems like a lot of time and work just for taking joyrides." Cyndi shifted in her seat to look directly at him. "Or is it more than that?"

"Much more, Cyndi; it could eventually mean part of my livelihood. I don't know if this was mentioned to you, but the fire towers are being phased out in the belief that air-reconnaissance will be much more practical and effective, so I'm planning ahead. Now for our ride."

Tim pushed his foot against the pedal and the helicopter pivoted right, then shot up and forward as he gently pulled the control lever and pressed on the stick.

"This is exciting!" Cyndi exclaimed as they skimmed along at almost eighty miles an hour not far above the treetops. Then a frightening thought hit her.

"This helicopter looked like it has only one engine. What happens if it fails?"

"If we were in a single-engine plane, we'd crash into that tangle of trees, one of the farms, or perhaps one of those little towns," Tim studied, not really answering her question yet.

Cyndi's stomach felt queezy just thinking about it.

"But with this whirlybird . . ." Tim continued. "Do you remember how we viewed the airport from over the clump of trees by my van?" While he was asking the question, he repeated that maneuver, pulling back on the stick while he pushed the lever down. They came to a stop in not much over one hundred feet.

"We can stop in this about three times as fast as a car on the highway," he explained.

"Yes, but we'd still be in the air." Cyndi still wasn't convinced of their safety.

Tim smiled. "If the engine actually quit and we had no more power from it, I'd push the pitch lever all the way down, putting the ship into autorotation as long as I let us down slowly. I'll explain it more later."

"All right," Cyndi conceded. "At least I feel better knowing you would be able to control it in that kind of emergency."

Tim clasped her hand in reassurance for a moment; then manipulating the stick lever sequence, he made the chopper rise higher and move forward again.

Cyndi watched the landscape drifting by beneath them. She had a wonderful, free sensation of floating in the air in spite of the sound of the motor.

Tim increased the speed back up to seventy-nine mph, but she felt more at ease than before and was thoroughly enjoying the ride, confident in Tim's ability.

He pointed out various spots below as they glided along,

his feet resting lightly on the pedals, the stick held between his thumb and one finger. Farms and several small towns passed below before the main forest; then a fire tower came into view ahead.

"Redbud?" Cyndi pointed in its direction.

Tim nodded, and when they were almost above it, they hovered a few moments before he pushed the stick slowly to one side, putting them into a wide, banking turn, circling over Cyndi's area.

When they changed direction, traveling north from the tower, Cyndi recalled the lights in that general area, the radio conversations, the crumpled map. She had almost convinced herself to mention them to Tim when he spoke as the helicopter turned west.

"I'll take you over my Walnut Ridge tower before we look at your grandfather's farm. Then we'll go over my home and the gristmill on our way back."

When they were again over the airport, Tim pushed the control stick forward. Cyndi drew in her breath and grabbed the seat as they suddenly lost altitude and seemed to be diving toward the ground. But in what she felt was just in time, he pulled back on the stick, pushed the lever, and they were suspended in the air.

She shot her gaze back out the window and found that they were settling down easily in the space by the hangar.

"That last move was so smooth, I didn't even feel the skids touch the ground," she said. "It was a great ride, Tim. Thanks for an exciting experience."

On the drive back to the tower, Tim glanced at Cyndi. "Since you had to provide your own lunch after I'd invited you out, would you be interested in my making up for it next weekend at the little restaurant in Milltown we went to once before?"

"Sure, I would. When?"

"Does Friday after we close the towers sound okay?"

"That's fine with me, Tim. It'll be fun." Cyndi's eyes sparkled with enthusiasm.

Friday morning before she left for the tower, she laid out the outfit she planned to wear so she wouldn't keep Tim waiting.

That evening she knew she looked pretty in the white, blue-flowered dress she'd chosen. Tim's smile of approval confirmed it as he escorted her to his van.

His black suit jacket fit him well and with his black jeans he seemed taller and slimmer than Cyndi had noticed before. She felt happy walking across the parking lot to the restaurant with him.

"Bertha's has always been a pleasant spot for a meal," he said. "The rowdy crowd never comes here. They hang out down at Pete's Grill, which is a blessing for Bertha."

"How does Pete feel about that?" Cyndi wondered.

"I really don't know," Tim chuckled. "But as far as I know, he doesn't discourage it."

While they were enjoying their grilled fish and baked potatoes, Cyndi's thoughts turned to the helicopter ride. "You said the Forest Service is planning to phase out the fire towers and substitute helicopters for detecting fires. When are they going to do this?"

"Already are. Some of the states have made the transition and have found that it works very well."

"Does that mean the towers will be abandoned?" Cynthia didn't really want to hear the answer.

"I understand a few will be used as lookout towers for the recreational use of the public." His voice was subdued. "The others are to be dismantled."

"Even though I hadn't planned to work there very long, I'll miss that old tower," she said, gazing absently at her plate.

"Me, too," Tim agreed. "You get an awareness of nature

up there that you experience nowhere else."

Later, when the waitress had brought blueberry pie topped with ice cream, Cyndi remarked, "I've been glad there haven't been any fires in the forest around here recently."

"We rarely have them once the trees have leafed out and the grass and bushes are green." Tim forked a bite of pie and continued. "But we did have fires recently—two in fact, this week. Rather strange ones the guys said."

"Strange? In what way?" Cyndi was immediately curious.

"Mainly that they started at all. And when. They both seem to have started about nine o'clock at night and spread rapidly as though they had been deliberately set."

Cyndi felt a prickling at the back of her neck. "Where were they located, Tim?"

"Over in the south area of Putnum, near the old unused Tiberville Trail that leads to the boundary.

"The one Monday night was several miles due north of Redbud; Wednesday's was west of the other one. It's possible we have a firebug around here. I sure hope not."

Cyndi said nothing about the incidents she thought might be connected to the fires. "Was anyone injured, Tim?" she asked quietly.

"No. They got the fires out quickly in each case," he assured her. "They were both in areas that had burned in recent years and consisted mostly of underbrush and young saplings. We hate to lose those areas, though, because they're fine for wildlife and eventually future timber. But they'll recover, and some reseeding may be done this fall."

Cyndi decided that if another such fire occurred, she was definitely going to tell Tim or Jeff what she'd observed—whether she sounded silly for being suspicious or not.

Tim was to be especially busy with the extra duties of the farm for a while, so except for a few short tower calls from him, the following weeks for Cyndi consisted only of the usual routine of study, daily chores, and tower duty until Saturday night of the second week when Jeff phoned.

"Lucio is planning to be in Milltown next weekend in order to be with Jennifer for the July Fourth picnic and fireworks. His sister has said I'm welcome to spend the time with them, too. Would you care to be my date for the festivities?"

"That sounds like fun, Jeff. Even though that's a holiday, I thought I'd spend some time in the tower during the morning if the sun isn't too hot. I'm doing some sketching from that angle. What time had you planned for?"

"I didn't know you were an artist, Cyndi!"

"Oh, I'm not really, but I do enjoy drawing and painting once in a while, and I haven't taken time for it since I've been here because of my study load," she explained, slightly embarrassed.

"Would it be convenient if I stop by your house at two o'clock on the Fourth? Lucio said the picnic dinner wasn't scheduled until quite late in the afternoon following the games and contests for the kids."

"Two o'clock will be fine, Jeff. I'll call Carlita to see what I can bring."

Tim phoned midweek to invite her to the Fourth of July picnic and she had to tell him she already had a date for it. Her disappointment was echoed in his voice when he said, "Okay, Cyndi; have a nice time. I'll talk to you again later."

It rained all day on the third, so Cyndi spent the day studying at Grandpa's home and sketching the bouquet of peonies she had arranged on the kitchen table.

The Fourth dawned clear, so Cyndi went to the tower at midmorning. It looked like fine weather for the outings in their area.

But there was an hour of heavy, gusty wind late in the

morning as the edge of a storm passed to the east. Cyndi had hurriedly swung down the tower windows and fastened them against the heavy indraft, glad that the phone was in its accustomed spot on the floor where it couldn't be blown off and damaged.

By noon the wind had softened to a pleasant breeze, and she reopened one of the windows, deciding to continue sketching until a little after one o'clock since everything was ready at home.

Because Cyndi had an abundance of eggs on hand, Carlita had suggested she make desserts, so two maple-custard pies were chilling in the refrigerator and two angel food cakes, one chocolate covered, the other, with cherries scattered through it and topped with fluffy white frosting, stood ready on the table.

Her clothes were ready too, so she would need time only to shower and change. At one-fifteen, Cyndi closed and latched the window, accidentally knocking her sketchpad onto the floor. As she stooped to pick it up, she saw something she hadn't noticed earlier under the chair. Wondering what she could have missed in her sweeping when she was last up there two days before, she peered closely at it. The object was a half-smoked cigarette.

Someone's been up here! No one has any business here but me; who could it have been? A faint chill swept through Cyndi as the map with two areas and her tower marked in red flashed into her mind.

Maybe there really was a connection, she thought, shoving her sketchpad and pencils into her tote. Hurriedly leaving the cabin, easing the door down on her back as quickly as possible, she secured it above her, then turned to go down the long flights of stairs.

Suddenly the sole of her right shoe landed on something that rolled, her hands missed the railings, and she skidded downward on her back. She screamed.

6

Grabbing frantically at the railing as she skidded, Cynthia stopped abruptly when she hit the first landing where the stairs made a turn.

In the seconds that followed, she realized what probably happened. The pen she had dropped from her tote a week or so ago must have stuck in a groove at the edge of the step, then been dislodged by the strong winds that morning.

Cyndi was bruised and shaken but didn't think she had broken anything. Her right ankle hurt intensely, and she couldn't put any weight on that leg without crying out in pain.

"What am I going to do now?" she cried in disgust.

Amazingly, her tote strap had stayed hooked in the bend of her elbow, so at least she needn't be concerned about that. She decided to crawl back up into the tower and phone Jeff at Carlita's home. The phone at the other end rang and rang with no answer. Guessing they must already be at the park, she dialed Tim's tower but got no answer there, either.

Standing brought tears to her eyes, so she tried Carlita's number again several times, waited awhile, then tried once more. She tried Tim's home number only once because she knew his dad was confined to bed.

Crawling over to the door, she pulled it up and eased herself down onto the step in a sitting position. "Well, here goes," Cyndi muttered and proceeded slowly down the stairs, sitting on each step in turn, gripping the railing above her head on each side, and holding the injured leg straight out in front of her.

By the time she reached the last of the hundred and twenty-three steps, her ankle was aching even worse. She sat there rubbing it, considering how best to get to her car.

Guess it's either crawl or stay here, she thought, glad she had jeans on and hadn't dressed for the day's special outing. At least something had worked out right, she decided ruefully.

She had just reached her car and was on her knees, reaching up to put the key in the door when she heard a car approaching. She turned to see Jennifer's convertible pulling in beside her with Jeff at the wheel. He jumped out, concern on his face.

"Cyndi, what's wrong? What happened?" Without waiting for an answer, he opened the convertible's door on the passenger side, then ran around and picked her up and put her on the seat.

"Me, Jane; you, Tarzan," was her attempt at humor. Then, "Seriously, Jeff, thank you. I appreciate the help."

He shut her door and got into the driver's seat. Backing and turning the convertible, he said, "Now, what happened to you? When I didn't find you at home, I thought maybe you'd forgotten the time."

"No, I hadn't forgotten, Jeff. I was in too much of a hurry and slipped on the tower stairs."

"Are you badly hurt? Should I take you to a doctor?"

"No. I just turned my ankle. I doubt that it's seriously hurt, but I can't stand on it very well."

"That's happened to me," he sympathized, "so I know how painful a sprain can be. We'll put ice on the ankle; that should help a little."

"I'm sorry I've caused a problem, Jeff. You can just drop me off at home. I'll be able to take care of it myself."

"You're no problem, Cyndi," Jeff smiled at her. "And I want you to come with me, unless you feel too bad. We'll drive by the park and get Jennifer or Carlita to help you with whatever you need to do before we go back for the fun."

Lucio and Jennifer were sitting together on a bench near the park entrance and both insisted on going with them to help however they could.

"Before we leave town, go past Carlita's house and we'll borrow Grandma's canes," Lucio suggested. "I rented a wheelchair for the day so she wouldn't refuse to go along, thinking she was a burden because she needs help."

He smiled at Cyndi. "We've never considered it that way, and we don't want you feeling that way, either. Understand?"

"I understand." Cyndi answered, aware that her friends were sincere.

While Lucio was in the Hernandez home getting the canes, Cyndi was considering whether she ought to mention the tower visitor to him and Jeff or just ignore the fear that it might have been more than an overly curious hiker.

When they arrived at her grandfather's home, the men insisted on making a chair of sorts with their crossed hands clasped together, carrying her inside and depositing her on the edge of the bed.

"I feel like a queen in her sedan chair," Cyndi giggled. "Now if you two will get the desserts from the kitchen, I'll have Jennifer get my things from upstairs so I can fix myself up a little."

By the time Jennifer had returned, Jeff was back with ice cubes wrapped in a washcloth to put on the injured ankle. "Fasten this some way after you've changed clothes, so it can be kept there for a while," he instructed her protectively. "It should make you more comfortable. Lucio and I'll wait on the porch; there's no hurry."

When Cyndi hobbled out on the porch, refusing their assistance except for getting down the steps, Lucio said, "You sure you don't want us to carry you back to the car?"

"No. I can make it all right. At least I'm going to try," she answered, gripping the canes and wincing every time she stepped on her right foot. "Did you find the pies and cakes in the kitchen?"

"Everything's stowed in the trunk," Lucio said.

"Guess we're ready then." Jennifer climbed in beside Cyndi, and they were soon nearing the outskirts of Milltown.

At the park, clusters of people strolled along the paths or sat on benches chatting together, watching exuberant youngsters shouting and laughing in play on the grassy areas and adjoining playground.

"Looks like folks are getting impatient for the softball game." Lucio waved toward the end of the park where bleachers were beginning to fill.

"Something smells wonderful." Cyndi sniffed, the aromas drifting from several areas in the pine grove where laden picnic tables could be seen among the trees.

"We'll take these things over to Carlita's table before checking out the pre-game practice," Lucio said, getting the pie hamper from the trunk and handing the cake carriers to Jeff and Jennifer.

Al was barbecuing whole chickens on the grill, painting them lavishly with a spicy-smelling sauce. In the middle of the grove, several men were watching an entire hog turning slowly on a spit over a pit of glowing coals.

"Besides the nice company, Jeff, I want to thank you for inviting me to enjoy these great aromas," she laughed.

"Wait till you taste the food." Lucio rolled his dark eyes. "Abuelita Evetia," he added, going over to give her a hug where she sat in the wheelchair good-naturedly directing Al in his cooking, "those tiny tortillas you made are for snacking ahead of time, aren't they?"

"You're always ready to eat," she chided, laughing and giving him a playful tap. "Even now when you're a man, what an appetite! I made them especially for you so enjoy them whenever you like."

Little Luz had been playing around an ice-filled tub

holding a watermelon, but came running when she saw Uncle Lucio passing the tray of appetizers. "Me, too!" she cried, scrambling up on the bench.

Later while Evetia was watching Luz at the playground, and the three young women were leisurely preparing fresh salad, chatting together, Carlita confided, "I'm afraid Juan won't do well in the game. He didn't seem his usual happy self this morning at breakfast."

"Probably was tense," Jennifer said. "It's understandable, playing in a special game like this one. He knows his team depends on him for extra runs."

"I know. He's to pitch most of the game, too." Carlita tried not to sound worried. "Maybe it's just a mother's concern, but he didn't even seem to be looking forward to tonight."

"Where is he? I haven't seen him," Cyndi remarked. "Or is practice about to begin?"

"He's around the park somewhere with his new friend, Dan Zodest," Carlita answered. "Warm-up's not to start for about half an hour."

"Shouldn't we get ready to walk over there?" Cyndi looked up from the lettuce she was working on. "I'm sure you want to have a good seat in the cheering section."

Jennifer spoke up. "I thought maybe you and I could stay here and tend the grill, Cyndi, especially since your ankle is hurting."

Cyndi nodded her thanks, not anticipating sitting on a bench in the late afternoon sun. She looked at Al with a grin, "Do you trust us to finish the chickens correctly?"

"Sure do," he smiled, laying aside the sauce-brush and tongs. Removing his long white apron, he handed it to Jennifer with a flourish. "Turn and baste each chicken every half hour. There's extra sauce in the ice-chest if you need it, also hot dogs and hamburgers you can start later around the edge of the grill."

Cyndi and Jennifer could hear the shouts and cheering from the crowded bleachers at the far end of the park. But in the picnic grove it was quiet except for the conversations of women fixing food or busy with other activities.

The sun was getting low in the western sky when the yelling stopped and the crowd trooped back across the park to the supper area.

Cyndi noticed that Juan appeared dejected. His family encouraged him on his performance when they gathered around the long table. Carlita shook her head sadly at the two young women as they poured tall glasses of cold lemonade and passed them around to the places at the table.

Twilight was falling by the time the empty watermelon tub and hampers were put in the back of the Hernandez station wagon.

"Alfredito," Evetia said, "I would like to go home. Luz can come with me, and you and Carlita will be a little more free this evening."

"But, Abuelita, the fireworks!" Carlita said.

"We shall watch from my window." Evetia calmly folded her hands on her lap. "We're not so far from the park that I can't see fine from there. I did so the year Luz was a tiny baby, remember?"

"All right, Abuelita," Al conceded. "Come on, Luz honey, into the car to go see the pretty fireworks." He pushed Evetia's wheelchair to the car and helped her into the front seat.

"Cyndi, since Mrs. Hernandez won't be using this chair tonight, how about me pushing you to where we want to go in the park?" Jeff asked.

"I'll do okay, Jeff; my ankle feels better already."

"It won't stay that way if you put too much strain on it," Jennifer warned. "Use the chair and be comfortable."

Cyndi smiled her answer, handing the canes to Lucio to return to his grandmother.

"You four go ahead and find a nice viewing spot," Carlita told them, not wanting to detain them. "Al and I'll be back by the time the display starts."

When they were settled in a comfortable spot at the edge of the large open area, Jennifer said, "Okay, Cyndi, now tell us. Why so mysterious about how you turned your ankle?"

Hesitantly at first, not wanting to appear overly dramatic, Cyndi recounted the incidents of the radio conversations and finding the portion of map.

Although Jennifer was obviously enjoying the mystery of it all, Cyndi noticed both Jeff and Lucio listening intently. "Have you mentioned this to anyone else?" Lucio questioned.

"No; frankly, I thought I might be reading something into it that wasn't true. At first, that is."

"What do you mean, at first?" Jeff asked.

"Before the fires two weeks ago," Cyndi answered.

"I didn't know we'd had fires here." Jennifer sounded surprised.

"They weren't close to Milltown," Cyndi explained. "I'm not sure, but I think they were in or near the areas marked on the map I found."

"Do you still have the map?" Jeff asked anxiously.

Cyndi nodded. "It's at home."

"This *is* mysterious," Jennifer said. "But how does it connect with hurting your ankle? You weren't fighting the fire, were you?"

"No." Cyndi proceeded to tell them about the cigarette in the tower and her subsequent fall.

"Is the cigarette still there?" Lucio asked.

"Yes. I didn't touch it," Cyndi assured him. "I realize it was silly of me to be afraid, because there obviously wasn't anyone around then. But I was very uneasy and acted carelessly."

"Oh, look!" Jennifer pointed to a pair of Roman candles flashing out their sparkling colors against the darkening sky. Then sky rockets followed one after the other, spreading ignited powders like fountains of colored jewels above them.

Cyndi noticed a tall, lanky figure with several chattering youngsters in tow settling on the grass not far from her little group. Lucio evidently saw them at the same time.

"Tim!" he called. "Over here."

When Tim reached them, Lucio introduced him. After shaking Jeff's hand, Tim squatted down by Cyndi's wheelchair. "Cyndi and I are tower buddies," he said to the others. Then to her, "What happened to you?"

"It's not nearly as serious as it looks," she answered, laughing lightly. "I got in a hurry and slid down a flight of tower stairs. Just turned my ankle, that's all."

"And we're pampering her," Lucio gave her an affectionate grin.

"Try to be more careful, Cyndi," he cautioned, and even in the dusk she could detect the deep concern in his blue eyes. Then standing, he said, "Nice to meet you, Jeff. I'll see the rest of you another time," and sauntered back to where the youngsters sat exclaiming over the continuing showers of lights and loud explosions.

"Always a Good Samaritan and Big Brother, that Tim," Lucio said. "It's a wonder some nice girl hasn't found out yet what a great husband he'll make. However, young lady," he added with a light laugh, putting his arm around Jennifer's shoulders, "I'm glad *you* didn't notice his attributes."

"Who says I didn't, Lucio?" she teased. "I just somehow preferred you!" He responded with a playful punch on her arm.

"Have you known him long?" Jeff asked. "Seems like a nice guy."

"Since we were in junior high," Lucio answered. "But I haven't seen him often in recent years. Those kids are from his Sunday school class. I saw them together at Christmas when I was visiting my family. Carlita said he tries to be a special friend to the ones who are without fathers or whose parents don't make an effort to spend time with them."

Good for you, Ace, Cyndi applauded silently.

Soft rain showers filled most of the next few days, so except for tending to the chickens, Cyndi stayed indoors studying and sketching, giving her ankle a rest.

She was glad she didn't need to drive anywhere. Grandpa had told her to use the things he'd stored, and the large walk-in pantry had jars of home-canned fruits and vegetables, as well as flour, sugar, cornmeal, and beans, each in a large covered ceramic crock. A neighbor left containers of milk on the porch every few days, and Cyndi had found the root cellar well stocked with root vegetables and apples. She knew there would be no need to visit the supermarket in town unless she wanted more coffee or tea.

The weather finally cleared by Saturday morning, bringing out the bright, warm sunshine. The sky looked newly washed, blue and cloudless. Tired of being confined to the house and with her ankle seeming stronger, Cyndi decided to drive to the general area of the mill and check through the surrounding forest, hoping to find evidence of other old buildings.

She drove past the turnoff where she and Tim had picnicked, from which the path led directly to the mill, but didn't find another road leading in that direction. Half a mile farther on, she noticed what appeared to be vehicle tracks leading across the edge of a meadow to a woods beyond. Since there was no ditch or fence to contend with, she decided to follow it.

In spite of the recent rain, the ground was firm and her car moved easily over the green growth of new grasses mixed with last year's dry stalks and leaves. The tire tracks led along an old hedgerow of crabapple trees and tangles of wild roses.

Although the faint trail continued on through the trees, Cyndi parked just at the edge of the wooded area in the shade of a large oak tree. She checked the ample pockets of the light jacket she'd worn over her jeans: apple, peanuts, colored pencils, sketch pad. She hadn't taken sketching supplies along the times she'd gone to the mill, and she didn't want to miss another good opportunity.

Getting out of the car, she followed the faint trail of compressed grass among the trees. After a while, her ankle began to hurt and she decided she might as well turn back as this was probably just a farmer's route between highways. Just then, rounding a clump of tall bushes, she found herself at the edge of a large clearing.

She saw that trees had been cut down and rolled to the edges of the field and the ground had been worked fairly recently. Two types of young plants had emerged and were growing well together; she thought the larger ones were probably corn. Deciding there must be a home nearby, Cyndi skirted the entire field but didn't find a road or even a path leading from the planted area except the one she'd followed.

Mystified, she dropped to one of the logs in a shaded area. *What an odd place for a cornfield,* she thought; *especially when it had to be cleared before planting.* Taking out the sketch pad, Cyndi munched an apple while gazing around the clearing, deciding what to sketch first.

She had just flipped the pad to a clean page after completing one drawing of graceful young plants when a twig snapped behind her with a resounding crack. Startled, she turned.

The man standing behind her was of medium height, about forty, his dark nondescript hair touched with gray, his face tense. The huge rifle he held was aimed directly at her, only a few feet from her head.

7

"What you doing, snooping around here?" he bellowed rudely.

"I'm not; I'm just drawing," Cyndi quavered, holding the sketch pad against her chest with crossed arms as though to protect herself.

"Why you way back in here? I saw you walking all around the—the garden," the man persisted.

"I was hoping to find another path or road leading to the old mill." It took all her strength to remain calm.

"Don't know anything about any mill, but you better not come in here again. We don't like folks nosing around."

"I'm sorry," Cyndi said. "I wasn't meaning to trespass. Would you please turn your gun away from me?"

"Uh, yeah. Was just out hunting. Hope you won't say nothing about this to anybody 'cause I didn't mean to scare you." He let the barrel drop but held the firearm awkwardly.

Cyndi stood and turned to face him, not answering him, very uneasy and not believing his excuse.

"What you doing with that paper and pencil?" he asked.

"I carry them with me to sketch trees and flowers, things that interest me." She just wished he would leave. But when he reached out as though to take the pad from her, she said quickly, "How about sketching you! Would you like a drawing of yourself?"

He looked uncertainly at her, taken aback by the question. Then, a normal ego curiosity getting the better of him, he said, "Sure, why not. What you want me to do?"

"Stand there just as you are. It'll only take a minute," she said, folding another sheet out of the way.

Cyndi's pencil moved quickly over the paper, bringing out the man's features, his stance, with a minimum of strokes. Then she carefully went over the sketch, pressing firmly with the pencil, making each stroke more distinct. "There you are," she said, tearing the page from the pad. "Fairly close resemblance, isn't it?"

"Not bad," the man said, his smile sincere this time. "Thanks, and remember, don't mention meeting me to anyone."

Cyndi smiled back without answering and hurried toward the bushes where the trail had ended. Walking quickly from the area, she wondered if he was watching her.

Her ankle was beginning to hurt as she hiked back to her car. Limping and wincing the last steps, she was relieved to get inside and sit down.

She sat a minute, curious about the encounter. Then starting the car, she drove back along the edge of the meadow to the road, wondering why the stranger had been so nervous about finding her there. *I hadn't thought about the possibility of wandering onto private property*, she thought. *I'll have to be more careful. But he acted as though I were inside a walled estate instead of an open field, pointing that gun the way he did.*

At church the next day, Cyndi looked around for Tim but didn't see him. After the service as she was visiting with Carlita, she remarked, "Lucio said my friend, Tim Nichols, attended here, but I haven't seen him."

"Church camp started yesterday in the northern part of the state," Carlita said. "Tim's there with the youngsters from his class." She reached down to take Luz's hand, worry creasing her brow. "The camp is for boys Juan's age also, and he had planned for it all winter, but now he has no interest at all in going and won't say why. He doesn't seem interested in talking about his new job with Dan's father, either. He started a week early since he didn't go to camp, but the enthusiasm he had is gone."

"Maybe he's not feeling well . . . Maybe he's depressed about something he doesn't want to trouble you with," Cynthia offered, trying to comfort her.

"I just don't know," Carlita said. "He says everything is fine, but he's not my energetic, happy Juan."

Cyndi drove home from church feeling very lonely. Carlita had invited her to spend the afternoon with them, but she had declined because of Carlita's concern over Juan. She knew it would make him uncomfortable if his parents wanted to have a talk with him and she were there.

At midweek when the weather was calm and radio projections from the national bureau had predicted more of the same, Cyndi was surprised when a storm suddenly blew in late one night. Startled by a loud clap of thunder, she jumped up to close the window.

A jagged streak of lightning cutting down from the sky was followed by a deafening roll of thunder. From somewhere very close to the house came a loud tearing sound, an ear-splitting crash. Because rain immediately fell in torrents, Cyndi decided she would have to wait until morning to investigate and crawled back into bed.

As suddenly as it had begun the storm passed; first the thunder rolls faded into the distance, and a short time later the rain ceased. Cyndi reopened her window to the wet coolness, hearing the heavy dripping of water from the trees.

She went to the other upstairs rooms to peer out the windows, trying to figure out what had caused the crash. But the darkness prevented her from distinguishing much at all except the distorted shape in the drive that identified her car.

Early the next morning after dressing in jeans and sneakers and a light sweatshirt, Cyndi went out the back door to take care of the chickens and check for damage. Noticing nothing amiss there or at the back of the house, she hurried around to the front, sure the damage must be there. Then she saw it.

A large branch the size of a tree had been torn from the giant oak near the end of the drive. Like an open umbrella, its mass of leafy boughs shielded her car from view.

"Oh, no!" she cried aloud. In a rush the previous day, she hadn't taken time to drive her car back into Grandpa's parking area in the barn. "It's your own fault," she berated herself, running across the wet grass to the fallen limb. Prepared to face a damaged automobile, she was cheered to find the huge limb stretched across the drive with only its long leafy boughs forming a wet, green prison for her car.

Cyndi pushed some branches out of the way, trying to assess the damage. She succeeded only in shaking off the water, which splashed on her head and down her face to the back of her neck into her sweatshirt.

Shivering, she thankfully noted that except for a smashed taillight and dent in the trunk, the only harm seemed to be scratched paint.

While eating breakfast, she pondered how best to move the obstruction off her car and from the driveway. Because of wide, perennial flower beds and bushes lining both sides, she didn't feel she should try to drive around the barrier even if she succeeded in removing the branch from the car. She remembered Grandpa had a workshop in the barn years ago and hoped it was still stocked with tools.

Cyndi walked past the massive double doors on the big red barn to a smaller one at the side. Pulling back the long bolt, she stepped into the dimness of the large, open expanse. The sweet aroma of hay and straw and the bland smell of chicken feed penetrated the air, with the faint odor of long-gone cattle and horses that had once inhabited the stalls.

She went to the remembered room in the corner of the spacious barn and found a wide assortment of tools arranged on the walls. She chose a small ax she felt she could probably wield and a long-handled pruner of a type her dad used. Confused about the many saws, not wanting to damage one by using it incorrectly, she finally took a rather small curved one with medium teeth.

Enjoying the atmosphere of the room, its faint aroma of wood chips and paints, the memory of toys Grandpa had fashioned there from leftover chunks of wood, she unfolded a burlap bag from a pile on the shelf. Into it she put a large chunk of wood from the crate under the worktable, a pair of canvas gloves, and the tools she had selected.

Sure wish David were here to help me, or that Jeff or Tim were in town, she thought as she selected a piece of two-by-four about as long as she was tall from those standing in a corner. Lugging the bag and the length of lumber back to her car, she used the pruner to sever the leafy boughs from the fallen limb. Cyndi found the green wood difficult to saw when she began working through the smaller branches lying on the car, but she finally completed the job and dragged the debris down the drive to an open spot by the barn.

Then she drove forward, parking the car well away from the fallen limb and turned her attention to the heavier limbs. After much inexperienced hacking with the ax, she finally got those loose, too, and dragged them to the pile with the others.

Cyndi was perspiring heavily now and feeling very uncomfortable from the leaves and chips sticking to her neck and face. More than anything right then, she wanted to shower and change clothes, but she still had the giant limb itself to move across the drive.

Sighing, she took a break, going for a glass of lemonade. She sat on the front steps, sipping the cool beverage and wishing she could just lift one end of the thing and pivot it off the drive without doing more damage to the gardens, but she knew it was much too heavy to attempt. She decided to try the old fulcrum-roll, the name she and David had given to a job-turned-game one year when they helped their dad clear large rocks from a field he wanted to make into a garden.

She put her empty glass on the wide porch railing, then set the block of wood on the ground near the end of the log that jutted onto the lawn. With the ax, she shaped one end of the two-by-four into a wedge, which she inserted under the log, resting it on the wood block. As she pushed her weight down on the other end, the log lifted a bit causing it to roll a short way. Cyndi continued the maneuver, repositioning the block each time until the log was off the drive and lay on the grass near the immense oak from which the lightning had torn it. Her body ached but she felt gratified by a job well done.

After cleaning up and eating just an apple for lunch, she stretched out on her bed and fell asleep. Cyndi dreamed of her sketchbook and the stranger with the rifle. Upon waking, she took a charcoal stick from her drawing case and rubbed it over the entire sheet of paper that had been directly under that sketch. As she moved it firmly over the surface, the man's features appeared, the lines white against the dark of the charcoal background she was making. "Just as I remembered him," she mused, removing the sheet from the pad and slipping it into the folder with other recent sketches.

Saturday evening Tim phoned. "If you're not already booked up for tomorrow, would you be interested in attending church with me and having a picnic afterward?" he asked.

"I have no plans," Cyndi answered happily, "and yours sound just right for tomorrow. What should I make for the picnic?"

"If you have time to fix a dessert and beverage, I'll bring the rest," he said.

Sunday morning, Rev. Mellinger's sermon caused Cyndi

to again reexamine the lifestyle she had been planning in recent years, her desire to earn a great deal of money for accumulating all the things she felt made for a good life. Because she had been thinking about this since resuming daily Bible reading and prayer, the pastor's words deeply impressed her. Near the end of his talk he encouraged the congregation to keep a few verses fresh in their minds. First from Ecclesiastes 5:19 and 20:

> To enjoy your work and to accept your lot
> in life,
> That is indeed a gift from God.
> The person who does that will not need to look back
> with sorrow on his past,
> For God gives him joy.

The minister turned the pages of his Bible and continued. "Something else very important for Christians to consider is found in Proverbs 19:17." Cyndi listened quietly to the words.

> When you help the poor,
> You are lending to the Lord,
> And He pays wonderful interest on your loan.

Then just prior to the benediction, the pastor commented, "Remember always, in considering your assets, the important point is not how much you give to God but how much you keep for yourself."

8

Following the service, Tim's van took him and Cyndi down the Old Parson blacktop road out of town to their old mill picnic area. But instead of stopping at the usual spot, Tim went past it about half a mile, then drove between two masses of bushes tangled with wild grapevines.

Cyndi saw that they were now on an almost obliterated weed-overgrown road that appeared to have been covered with crumbled bark. "I hadn't noticed a road leading back in here when we came before," she commented.

"It's an entrance too well concealed for anyone to see unless they're scouting around on foot," Tim stated. "From what I've been able to figure while checking county history at the library, this was evidently one of the early roads following an even earlier Indian trail."

"I wonder why the new road wasn't constructed over it," Cyndi questioned.

"Probably didn't follow as direct a route as later road-builders determined was best to connect with main highways," Tim answered. "This was one of the old corduroy roads made from logs, which eventually deteriorated into what we see now." He drove the van off the bark path and under the drooping branches of a magnificent weeping willow tree.

When he shut the motor off, the sound of moving water reached Cyndi's ears and she asked, "Is that the mill stream I hear?"

"Yes. After it leaves the mill, it curves in a wide arc and passes behind that stand of birch trees over there." He pointed in that direction.

Together they spread a blanket on the grass beneath the long, graceful fronds of the willow. From high branches the airy greenery dipped its tips to within a few feet of the ground like a giant parasol forming a chamber of cool, filtered light, secluding them from the heat of the day.

Cyndi spread a yellow tablecloth across the center of the blanket and set out a plate of frosted raspberry tarts she'd made from a jar of Grandpa's preserves. Then while she filled tall glasses with iced lemonade, she watched Tim unwrap two large dishes.

"Fried chicken and potato salad!" she exclaimed. "How did you get those ready on such short notice?"

"Fixed the salad last night after I phoned you and fried the chicken early this morning." He grinned. "After Mom died, Dad and I both became fair cooks."

"Looks as though you're more than fair," Cyndi said admiringly.

Tim smiled his thanks, then bowed his head, praying aloud, "Heavenly Father, thank you for your abundant provision and for this beautiful day. Thank you too, Lord, for bringing Cyndi into my life. Amen."

Cyndi's heart skipped a beat at his last thank you; a light blush tinged her cheeks when she raised her head and their eyes met. She looked away immediately, feeling unaccountably flustered.

After a few moments, he said, "Here, Cyndi, let's see if you can stand my cooking." He handed her the blue bowl with crisp-looking chicken pieces nestled in white paper napkins.

The chicken proved to be as crunchy as it looked, yet moist and flavorful. The salad, lemonade, and tarts were delicious. Cyndi and Tim relished the meal, complimenting each other's contributions, delighting in being together.

"How about a walk over to the stream?" Tim suggested. "We'll put the dinner leftovers in the ice chest and eat them later."

Cyndi smiled happily. "I'd like that, Tim. It's such a beautiful day. It's fun to be here with you."

The sound of moving water was getting clearer and when they rounded the stand of birch trees, Cyndi saw the narrow stream sparkling in the sunlight.

"Nice here, isn't it?" Tim asked, reaching out to clasp her hand and lead her across a jumble of stones to a grassy area. He stopped at a pair of chair-size rocks beneath a willow tree almost as large as the one where they'd had their picnic.

"It's beautiful," Cyndi marveled, sitting on one of the smooth gray rocks. She reached down for a pebble and tossed it into the clear water; it landed with a soft plunk and tiny splash. She followed it with another. "It's so peaceful here, Tim. The people who lived at the mill must have loved this place."

Cyndi gazed across the stream to the tall green conifers, majestic against their background of a fifty-foot outcrop of rock in the hill that rose behind them. Above the countless shades of green in the landscape, fluffy baby clouds floated in a sky so blue it brought tears to Cyndi's eyes. She had never felt as happy and content as she did at that moment.

When she turned to smile at Tim, to share her enchantment, she met a look in his blue eyes, a tenderness in his countenance that caused a tightening in her throat and made her heart flutter. She couldn't seem to pull her gaze away and sought for something to say; nothing came to mind.

Then Tim smiled and stood, holding out his hand. "I'll show you one of my favorite spots. I discovered it as a teen."

They walked upstream a short way through wild grasses and scattered flowers to where the stream began its wide curve back toward the mill.

"The water is low right here this time of year," Tim said.

"Do you mind taking your shoes off and wading across?"

"Sounds like great fun!" Cyndi exclaimed with delight. "Are we carrying our shoes with us, or are we coming back this way?"

"We'll leave them here. I'll put them on that tree stump."

Cyndi slipped out of her shoes and bravely stepped into the stream's edge. The water was very cool even in the hot sun as it moved swiftly past her ankles.

Tim joined her, his bare feet large to match his tall frame, splashing droplets on her legs as he stepped into the water. "May be a bit uncomfortable in spots because of scattered stones on the stream bed, but there's no other way across unless we went all the way to the mill and backtracked. Also, I wanted you to see the opposite bank from this direction because it's blocked by brush, coming from the mill."

"I don't mind," Cyndi said good-naturedly; "I'm enjoying it."

Tim bent and rolled the legs of his slacks above his knees. "You may have to hold your skirt out of the way when we get to the middle of the stream."

"All right," she said, taking his offered hand. Sunlight dancing across the surface gave the cool, rushing water the appearance of a path of jewels.

When Cyndi stubbed her toe on a rock and would have fallen without Tim's firm grip, they burst into laughter like little children, continuing so across the stream, splashing each other with handfuls of glistening water.

Emerging on the other side, they stepped onto soil as sandy as an ocean beach. "I hadn't noticed the sandiness of the stream's other edge because of the rocks," Cyndi remarked, wriggling her toes in the dry grittiness, which was hot to her feet after the comfort of the water.

"Look here, Cyndi." Tim was pointing to indentations in damp sand at the water's edge. "A white-tailed deer brought her fawn here for a drink this morning."

Cyndi turned to look, glimpsing at the same time a bright turquoise dragonfly lighting on Tim's arm. She gasped at its slender, ethereal beauty. "Tim, look! Just look!" she whispered.

A few moments later he took her hand again, leading the way across the short expanse of sand, saying, "It's cooler over here."

"What's wrong?" he asked when Cyndi squealed and jumped aside.

"Just a small snake," she answered, laughing self-consciously. "I stepped on it."

"Probably scared him more than he did you," Tim chuckled. "He's probably headed for the coolness near the hill just like we are." He bent, peering into a clump of grass. "There he is, a young bull snake. He's harmless."

In a short time they were entering the shade cast by the hill. As they approached nearer, Cyndi saw that an immense slab of rock about twenty feet wide and forty feet high had at some time sheared loose from the hill's outcrop and dropped to the ground below. The top of the three-foot-thick slab leaned against the sheer rock face, its bottom resting about fifteen feet from the base of the hill forming a tent-like chamber.

"The sand here feels so cool," Cyndi said when they stood outside the entrance where tiny fragile ferns massed at the base of tall broad-leafed ones. "This is a beautiful place."

"I discovered it when I was thirteen and decided then I'd like to live here someday," Tim said.

"Inside the stone tepee?" Cyndi teased.

"No," Tim chuckled. "Although a person could, of course, during the summer. It's cool in there and rain doesn't drip through anywhere. This is part of the land connected with the gristmill. I decided I wanted the whole thing, not considering at that age where I could possibly get the money for it."

"Do you still?"

"Sure wouldn't mind," he admitted.

"Who owns it now? Are they living on it somewhere?"

"No. The people who inherited it years ago have just let it stand idle. They live in another state."

"It seems a shame for such a nice area not to be lived on and enjoyed, doesn't it?" Cyndi remarked.

"My sentiments exactly," Tim agreed. They stood together, their backs toward the hill, admiring the scenery.

"I want to show you another reason this place intrigues me so," he said, taking her hand and leading her into the tall spire-shaped opening between the rock wall and the sheared-off slab. It was cool inside; they stood a minute letting their eyes adjust to the gloom.

Cyndi saw a small stone-circled firepit in the hard packed sandy floor, and not far from the doorway a flat-topped boulder. After wiping it with her hand, she sat down.

Tim dropped cross-legged on the sand facing her. "I think that rock you're sitting on may have once been used as an anvil of sorts," he commented.

"Really?" Cyndi got up to look at it, then sat down again. "You mean someone used this as a workshop?"

"More likely a home." Tim took a small flashlight from his pocket, shining the beam on another large stone near the opposite wall. "See its concave surface; it was probably a grinding stone for grain."

"Why would they prepare grain that way with the mill so close?" she asked.

Tim chuckled. "They'd have lived here long before the mill was in existence, possibly before any white folks were in the area."

"You mean native Americans?"

"Yes, when I discovered this spot as a boy, the entrance was pretty much hidden by fallen rocks and brush. The more I investigated, the more it intrigued me. It still does."

"This small area has a lot of interesting history in it, doesn't it?" Cyndi remarked.

"Sure does. I'd like to be able to buy it someday and make it into a nature preserve. But right now I have a very slim wallet." Then he smiled at her. "You look so pretty sitting there, Cyndi. Do you enjoy these things?" He gestured toward their surroundings.

"Yes, I do." She bent to pick up several pebbles half buried in the sandy floor. "I was always collecting stones when I was young. Whenever I was around Grandma, she'd join me. I think she collected unusual ones as I did, though she always gave me the ones we found together."

"I have a few collections at home, too," Tim said. "I'd like to show them to you; would you have supper with Dad and me sometime soon? I'd very much like you two to meet."

"Oh, Tim, I think that would be great! Let's make it potluck; let me bring part of the meal."

"Just might do that," Tim grinned. "We'll discuss it in a week or so . . ."

They sat a long time talking about their families and childhoods. Cyndi told Tim of her early plans for great financial gain and the rethinking she'd done lately. They shared thoughts about the Lord and ideas on how He guides one's life.

When the sun was almost setting, they took a walk along the stream; as shadows lengthened and the sky became streaked with pink and gold, they returned to the van and had picnic leftovers for supper.

The evening was peaceful, quiet except for occasional chirpings and murmurings from small birds and animals.

"What's that noise, Tim?" Cyndi asked. "Sounds like a fingernail being pulled over a comb's teeth."

"A wood frog, a tiny coppery fellow with a Lone Ranger mask. Fits easily in my palm when I can catch one, but they shut right up when they sense you're trying to find them," Tim explained.

"You know so much about nature, Tim. What started your interest?"

"My mother. When I was very young, she began making me aware of the wild things—from insects to animals—helping me learn their habits and how to distinguish between them. She had noticed my interest and encouraged it."

Tim smiled at Cyndi through the dusk of early evening, a longing on his face for something he'd not yet attained. "I've never been able to forget that, Cyndi. It's as though it became a part of me."

9

When Tim took Cyndi home, they sat for a while on the front porch swing, its slow, rhythmic creaking accompanying the symphony of night sounds.

"It's been such a fun day, Tim," Cyndi whispered softly. "I wish it didn't have to end."

"Yes, it has," Tim agreed. "You added a lot to it for me. You know that, don't you?"

Cyndi nodded, then realizing he could barely see her in the dark, murmured, "Yes, Tim."

He clasped her hand in his, and they sat quietly for a few moments.

Tim broke the stillness. "I'll call you later this week about coming for dinner." Leaning over, he kissed her cheek and then walked to his car.

As the rumble of the motor faded into the distance, Cynthia continued to sit there, her feelings in turmoil, trying to deny the small tugging in her heart.

"Lord," she prayed, "I'm confused. Tim is such a nice person, Jeff too. I enjoy being with them, but I'm afraid to care about anyone in a special way again—for a while at least. Please guide my emotions, so I give my love only to the one you've planned for me. Amen." Cyndi began the slow creak, creak of the swing again and stayed there a long time, her thoughts flitting like the fireflies over the questions that had been bothering her lately.

Finally, when the moon rose high to begin its journey

across the starry sky, she went to bed, having resolved nothing but experiencing God's peace.

On Thursday Tim phoned to invite her to his home for Sunday dinner, saying he would stop by for her in time for the morning service.

When they entered the Nichols home shortly before noon, the delicious aroma of baking ham met them. Cyndi declined Tim's offer of a seat in the living room and followed him past a fully set dining room table to the kitchen where he slipped a pan of raised yeast rolls into the oven and turned the flame high under a kettle of water.

"Now I want you to meet Dad." He led her back through the dining room to a hall connecting with the bedrooms.

Even though Tim's dad was seated on the edge of the bed in a dressing gown, his hand gripping a nearby walker, Cynthia could see where Tim got his lankiness. Mr. Nichols' hair was salt-and-pepper waves. His dark eyes welcomed her as he held out his free hand when Tim introduced them. She noticed the wrinkles around his eyes when he smiled warmly at her.

"Pardon my not getting up, Cyndi. Seems to be taking forever for my hip to regain its strength." They chatted together a few minutes about Grandpa David; then Tim said, "Cyndi, if you'll slip the platter of corn into the kettle of boiling water, I'll help Dad to the table."

"Many's the time I had to help you onto your chair when you were a youngun, Tim," Marsh said to his son. "Guess the tables have turned on us, haven't they?"

During dinner Marsh asked about Cyndi's family. "Well," she began, "after my brother David and I graduated from high school, our parents followed through on something they'd secretly wanted to do for years. They joined a small group assisting an indigenous pastor in southern Mexico.

They felt we could get on fine, which we have. We were both able to find jobs that fit our college schedules.

"David just finished two years at a small Christian college. Because he wasn't sure what the Lord wanted him to do with his life, he took basic Bible courses with hands-on training in some manual skills, thinking these would prepare him for whatever line of work he went into."

"Did your family visit your grandparents here when you were young?" Marsh asked.

"Yes. I have fond memories of those few times," Cyndi answered. "They visited us once in Minnesota when I was in first grade," she added with a light laugh. "I wanted to take Grandpa to school with me for Show-and-Tell time. I wanted the other kids to see how he could take out his teeth and put them in again because I thought it was the neatest trick I'd ever seen."

The men laughed with her and Marsh said, "I guess dentures could look that way to children. Kids always have such a refreshing outlook on things. When Ace was about four, he asked where the fireflies bought such tiny batteries. His interest in nature started early."

The dinner hour progressed pleasantly. Afterward, when Marsh had been made comfortable on the living room couch, Cyndi joined Tim in cleaning up the kitchen. They hardly noticed the work because they had such a good time being together.

As they prepared a small tray for Marsh with after-dinner coffee and a second piece of pie, Tim said, "I'd like to show you some of my collections if you want to see them."

"Sure I want to, Tim," Cyndi said. "I've been looking forward to that."

He led the way to a door just off the living room; when he opened it and stepped aside for her to enter, she gasped. "I never expected this, Tim!" Opened white shutters at raised windows allowed the bright afternoon sun to light up the room.

"This was Mom's special place to get away to sew or read," Tim stated. "After she died Dad suggested I move these things in here—not only for my sake but in her memory because she got me started on my collections." Tim looked around the room as he talked, and Cyndi followed his gaze, taking in the narrow cabinets and counters surrounding the room under walls completely covered by framed collections of hundreds of butterflies and moths, and glass-doored cabinets.

"They're gorgeous, Tim, absolutely beautiful!" Cyndi said quietly, awestruck.

Tim smiled, slipping an arm around her shoulders, his joyous interest in these things evident on his face as he shared her delight in them. After a few minutes of watching her gaze move wonderingly over the myriads of colored designs, sizes, shapes of the beautiful creatures in the wall frames, Tim walked over to a stepstool and sat down.

"Browse to your heart's content, Cyndi, and ask about anything that especially interests you," he offered.

"Oh, everything here does, Tim! I visited a museum once, and I thought *that* was interesting, but it doesn't even compare with this display! And you have more in the cabinets?"

Tim nodded, grinning happily. "More of the same in those shallow drawers, plus there are fossils, rocks, and Indian artifacts in the cabinets."

"You collected them all yourself?" Cyndi still could hardly comprehend gathering that many specimens of fragile-winged creatures.

He nodded again. "All except a few things Mom helped me find when I was very young. They're marked with thin blue ribbons on their identity cards. The collection is large, but I've been working on it for about twenty years."

Cyndi and Tim spent the rest of the afternoon inspecting more of his collection. When the setting of the sun brought dusk to the room, they were reminded of the time.

While Tim wakened Marsh from his nap, Cyndi went to the kitchen to prepare sandwiches and lemonade. The three of them had supper together on trays in Marsh's room. As they ate, Cyndi realized how content and happy she was, glad for having shared this day with Tim.

Later as Tim was driving her home under a sky glistening with stars, he said, "Something we talked about earlier has been on my mind a lot, Cyndi: the pressing need you feel to have a lot of money."

"I remember," she said. "It's been on my mind lately, too."

"I decided to search the Bible and try to find something that might be helpful for you," Tim said.

"And did you?" Cyndi asked.

"Yes, two verses in Colossians: 'Don't spend your time worrying about things down here. . . . Don't worship the good things of this life; your real life is in Heaven.' And one in Proverbs along the same line: 'Don't weary yourself trying to become rich. Why waste your time? For riches can disappear as though they had the wings of a bird.' "

10

During the heat of August, Cyndi checked conditions daily at the tower but didn't have to spend a lot of time there; she had been instructed that dangerous fires were rare when trees and other growth were succulent and green. She was glad for leisurely time to study and sketch in Grandpa's big old house, which held the night's coolness during most of the day. But she wasn't anticipating the prospect of weeks stretching ahead with no fellowship except Sunday services. Jennifer was on a trip with her parents, and Tim had phoned a few days after her visit to his home, saying he wouldn't be around either.

"I'll be away for a few weeks, Cyndi. A neighbor will stop in every day to cook Dad's dinner and do a few chores. I expect to be back around the end of the month."

Cyndi phoned Carlita the next morning, setting up a few coffee-time and lunch dates for the coming weeks, then baked some cookies and took them to the Nichols home as a thank you to Tim's dad for the nice afternoon she'd spent there.

Then, quite unexpectedly, Cyndi found the month busy. Jeff had phoned the evening after her visit with Mr. Nichols.

"I'm going to be in Milltown most of August, Cyndi. If you have no objections, I'd like to spend some time with you. I want us to have a chance to really get to know each other."

The next few weeks were like a whirlwind courtship. She and Jeff spent many evenings in good-natured companionship, a few interesting day-long trips, dinner dates at fine restaurants, and pleasant drives under star-studded skies.

At the end of the month Jeff extended a special invitation. After telling her he was leaving Milltown the next day, he said, "I've arranged with my parents for a small house party in September. I want my folks to meet you, Cyndi. Jennifer and Lucio have already accepted. We'll drive to Chicago together on a Friday evening and you three would return Sunday night. Please say you'll come."

Completely surprised by the invitation and not at all sure she should agree to join them, or even if she wanted to, she hesitated.

"Cyndi, you will come, won't you?" Jeff entreated.

"I don't know, Jeff. Will you phone tomorrow before you leave? I'll tell you definitely then."

As she prepared for bed, Cyndi's thoughts were in a quandry. She wanted very much to go with Jeff, sure it would be an exciting weekend. A home like his undoubtedly would be a pleasure to visit, but going for the purpose of being presented to his parents was what bothered her. It sounded as though Jeff had more than friendship in mind; he'd been inferring as much several times lately, and she didn't want to consider something that serious just yet. Besides, there was Tim, and she hadn't sorted out her feelings for him yet.

As she had been doing on a regular basis lately, Cyndi knelt beside her bed for prayer. When she slipped between her cool sheets, thoughts about the house party returned. She lay quietly considering a number of things, thankful for the electric fan humming nearby in the unusually oppressive heat.

She had noticed several beautiful bright red leaves on the sassafras trees by the tower, a sign Tim had said meant autumn was near. She should have made definite plans about the school semester that was to start soon; she'd have to decide before talking to Jeff in the morning. And Grandpa was to phone the next night. She knew a lot rested on her decisions: an extended vacation for Grandpa, her eventual earning ability, possibly her entire future.

Cyndi restlessly pushed the sheet off her feet, flipped her pillow over, tossed and turned, thought and prayed. The illuminated dial of her little travel clock displayed two a.m. before she fell asleep. Having reached her decision, she slept soundly, peacefully.

The following morning, the radio weather forecast was for a cold front to move into the area with the possibility of tornados forming. Even so, Cyndi's voice was bright and happy when Jeff phoned for her answer.

"Yes, Jeff, I'll be happy to come. Please thank your mother for the invitation."

"That's great, Cyndi; see you soon."

That evening while Cyndi was preparing a light supper Jennifer phoned, excited about the coming visit to Jeff's home.

"I almost decided not to go," Cyndi confided. "But I had asked the Lord to guide my affections and finally realized I'd probably have to learn as much as possible about the men He brings into my life, and keep my mind and heart open for His leading."

"I think that's a wise decision," Jennifer said. "I've known several girls who rushed into engagements and marriage knowing almost nothing about the guy's background and family relationships, even his personality quirks. It can cause a lot of problems later in their lives."

"I've seen that happen, too," Cyndi agreed pensively. "It almost happened to me, but you certainly seem to have made a fine choice in Lucio."

"Yes, I'm so thankful and fortunate," Jennifer said fervently. "It pays to let God truly guide in our decisions."

The two young women chatted happily for a few more minutes, setting up a date for lunch and shopping late the following week. They'd decided to use that day together for choosing exactly what clothes to take on the house-party trip. It would be a way of life unfamiliar to both of them, but one which they were thrilled to experience.

11

The air held a tinge of coolness one morning in early September when Cyndi opened the tower window. Light fog lay upon higher levels of land, giving an appearance of chiffon veils floating softly over high rock outcroppings and among the tops of tree-covered hills. The haze disappeared by midmorning replaced by sheet clouds spreading across the sky.

When afternoon sunshine heated her high cabin, hundreds of wasps began gathering on the few closed windows. With her arm resting on the sill of an open window, Cyndi sat reading; she watched entranced as a wasp settled on her wrist and began preening itself like a kitten, licking its feet then washing its face. It was carefully going over its feelers when the phone rang. Cyndi gently pushed the insect away with a fingertip before answering the persistent ring.

"The sheet clouds have broken up into what is called a mackerel sky, Cyndi. Have you noticed the beauty of those little billows lined underneath by the low sun?" Tim sounded eager, happy. "It means we'll have a fine night. How about a picnic supper and a canoe ride on the gentle section of the millstream?"

"Sounds great, Tim. It's good to hear your voice. When did you get back?"

"Late yesterday. I'll have the food ready, so just bring tableware and a thermos of coffee. I'll be by about seven-thirty."

The evening *was* beautiful as Tim had predicted. Fluorescent tints streaked the western sky while Tim and Cyndi enjoyed their picnic at a new spot. When the colors faded into approaching dusk, they stood beside the rushing stream, watching a doe on the opposite bank drinking from the water gurgling over the rocks.

When the deer had moved back among the saplings, Tim led Cyndi upstream to a group of young willows where a small canoe was moored.

He assisted her in, seating her in the little craft, untied it from a tree, pushed its bow from the sand, and deftly stepped in.

"You did that as gracefully as a dancer," Cyndi said with a light laugh. "If I had tried that, I'd have been in the water."

"Takes a little practice," Tim said humbly. "Can be an awkward move the first few times." After maneuvering the canoe to the stream's center, he used the paddle only as a rudder, guiding the little craft on the current that moved it slowly, silently along its dark liquid path. The air, mild against their faces, was becoming filled with gentle buzzings and twitterings of an Indian-summer evening.

As dusk settled deeper around them, small dots of light appeared on the water's surface. Cyndi looked up to discover stars already scattered over the darkening sky. The moon rose as the canoe followed the stream's wide arc through jack pine and hickory trees.

Although they couldn't see them in the darkness, the heavy fragrance from a trumpet vine filled the air when the quickening current carried them along. A little farther on, Tim expertly swung the craft toward shore, beached it on the edge of a sandy area, and fastened its mooring rope to the crotch of a fallen tree. The couple strolled down a series of paths back to the van.

On the drive home Tim said, "I'm flying to Indianapolis day after tomorrow to deliver some packages for Bartow, the fellow you saw in the airport office the day of our chopper ride. He's started a small delivery service; gives me an opportunity to earn some extra money. Would you care to go along? I'd very much like you to."

"What about the towers?" Cyndi asked.

"No problem; most things are still well greened. In another month we'll need to be on alert," Tim answered.

"In that case, I'd like to go, Tim. What time do we leave?"

"Early. How about seven-thirty? Dress comfortably for walking; thought we might take in a museum while we're there."

"Fine. Should we pack a lunch?" Cyndi asked.

"Could bring a thermos of something. It'll be nice having another day with you; I've missed you."

The next day was again unseasonably hot, the air oppressive, but nightfall brought a quick shower. Cyndi woke at dawn to the soft patter of raindrops dripping from the trees. Afraid Tim might cancel today's flight, she was relieved when he phoned at six to assure her everything was on schedule. Because no one was at that little airport office before six, he had filed his flight plan the night before and checked the plane for their early start.

On the drive to the airport Tim said, "You were right to be concerned about the weather possibly canceling our plans. It's something we can never take for granted. Whatever the conditions, we have to consider how it may change. The report last night said a front's approaching, but it's so far to the west, it shouldn't be a concern until early tomorrow, late tonight at the earliest."

"Why is a front a problem?" Cyndi asked.

"Isn't necessarily, but a front's passage always signals some change in the weather. Its severity depends a lot on the depression's activity and strength, also how far away its center is."

"There's more to consider before going up than I realized," Cyndi remarked as Tim turned the van into the airport road and parked near the office. She didn't see the helicopter anywhere, just a small red and white single-wing prop plane. She realized she was in for another new experience.

When they were in the air, climbing above scattered cloud cover, Cyndi marveled at how different everything was from her experience in the helicopter.

The two hours passed quickly. Landing the small craft at a small suburban airstrip, Tim transacted his business and rented the other man's car for the drive into the city.

They enjoyed brunch in a small restaurant followed by some shopping: special teas, a wheel of cheese, and hard candies for Cyndi; for Tim's dad, a few needed clothes, and aspirin for pain. Stopping for snack first, they went on to the museum and art gallery. Being together was comfortable and they often found themselves unconsciously walking hand-in-hand. About midafternoon Tim glanced at his watch for the third time in a short period.

"Guess we'd better be getting back, Cyndi. Fellow at the airport said the weather had gotten a little unstable earlier to the west, though there hadn't been any problems reported. Anyway, I'd just as soon start back well ahead of any foreseeable heavy changes. I want us to have a smooth trip home."

But Cyndi was far from encouraged when, as Tim assisted her into the little plane, they saw just off the far edge of the field the wreckage of a small aircraft.

"Be back in a few minutes," he said trying to hide the concern on his face.

When Tim returned he said nothing until they were in the air and the airport was far behind.

"I know seeing that must have upset you; it did me, too. Happened shortly after we left to drive into town. The pilot was from Louisville. He got caught in a low-altitude windshear, with no warning."

"The pilot, did he . . . ?" Cyndi was feeling very uneasy.

"He didn't make it, Cyndi, neither did his passenger," Tim answered quietly. "But I wouldn't have taken off if I'd had any doubts about our route. They rechecked afterward as far west as St. Louis, up to Chicago and over to South Bend; everything proved quiet. It was just one of the weather quirks that can't be anticipated at times far enough ahead, even with the most modern equipment at metropolitan airports."

The pleasure of the outgoing flight that morning was lost now. Cyndi's entire body seemed cramped with tenseness and she prayed almost mechanically as the distant landscape sped by far beneath them. How quickly a happy time could change to one of fear. Then she remembered she and Tim both belonged to the Lord; nothing could happen to them without His permission. She tried to relax a bit and closing her eyes prayed more calmly for their safety.

When she opened them, a thin bank of dark clouds was forming on the horizon ahead of them—just the opposite kind of sky she was hoping for.

"We'll have to change our course," Tim stated as winds began buffeting them. "A cloud change means changes in the weather, as you know, and this wind rise isn't encouraging. There may be only a trough, a small tongue of low pressure, but I don't dare take a chance. If the approaching storm is near our area when it's time to land, we could experience altimeter error as well as severe turbulence and wind shifts right down to the ground; it would be almost impossible to taxi this small plane.

"We'll fly to one side of what looks like a storm ahead," he continued, "and wait in clear air for it to pass by. We have plenty of extra gas for that, Cyndi, so don't be frightened."

"I'll try," Cyndi promised, not at all convinced she could carry it off.

Tim maneuvered so the cloud buildup was off to their

right rather than dead ahead, making Cyndi more at ease. Soon it had passed to a spot behind them and he began to bring the aircraft back in the general direction of the original course. The wind seemed to be decreasing, but clouds were beginning to form again. Glancing sideways, Cyndi noticed a look of concern on Tim's face, a tightening of his jaw.

Trying not to get too tense again herself, she continued praying silently for their safety, observing Tim's skillful handling of the controls. Then she saw the wide expanse of green below and asked, "Is that our forest?"

He nodded, "It won't be much longer. We're coming in from a different direction so the landmarks won't be familiar to you."

"You still look worried. Are you expecting problems?"

"We may be in for a rough jolt or two. How about holding that package of Dad's new clothes on your lap; it can serve as a cushion if we run into some turbulence."

While Cyndi picked up the package he continued, "Notice the ovoid shape of those stationary clouds, their clean-cut edges? They're a sure sign of great wind waves forming, usually to the lee of big ranges of hills like the ones we'll have ahead."

"Can't you go around the area like you did before?" she asked.

"Don't think I'd have sufficient fuel to do that again, Cyndi. But those clouds indicate the presence of torrents of air that can either drag a plane down or sweep it up to a great height. I'm telling you so you can be prepared in case we have a bumpy ride coming up."

A haze began to form in the air and visibility deteriorated rapidly, continuing to worsen until they could see almost nothing at all.

Where are you, Lord? Cyndi thought; *Are we going to be lost after all, like that pilot this morning?*

Hoping to sight something familiar to get his bearings,

Tim dropped the plane lower in a careful glide through an opening that had developed in the foggy cloud mass.

Like a phantom, the bold, impenetrable face of a rock outcropping rose before them.

"Help me, Lord!" Tim prayed desperately. "Protect your face, Cyndi!"

In the fraction of a second it took her to clasp the package against her lowered head, Cyndi's heart felt as though it were stopping, her held-in breath choking her.

When nothing happened in the next few seconds, she peered over the top of the package, through the windshield into the dense atmosphere. Tim had miraculously brought the plane's nose up and around just enough to clear the rocky bluff which was now outside the window to his left.

She was drawing a quick breath of relief when a sharp forceful gust of wind, like a giant unseen hand, jerked the craft suddenly upward, then even more quickly pushed it down and sideways, catching a wing against the rock face of the hill.

Cyndi heard herself scream as the wing sheared off and cockpit glass cracked as Tim's head crashed against it. Then they were spinning earthward in what seemed to be an endless slow-motion drop.

Cyndi pressed her face into Mr. Nichols' package just before they crashed through the tops of towering Virginia pines and ancient black-walnut trees. The plane seemed to be ripping apart. She felt herself flung across space, then searing pain and the welcome blackness of unconsciousness.

Cyndi woke to sensations of pain and the plaintive call of a mourning dove. She knew she should open her eyes but something deep inside, something frightening on the fringe of her memory, made her keep them tightly shut.

Finally she forced one eye partly open, surprised to find herself flat on her back looking up through the tangle of a bush to tall trees above. Unsure as to what she was doing there, she slowly untangled herself and got to her knees, rubbing the scratches on her arms and wincing at her aching body, especially the pain in her ankle.

Cyndi's legs were weak beneath her when she tried to stand. Her knees buckled, making her try twice before succeeding. Then a red piece of metal wedged between the leafy branches of a large rough-barked tree caught her gaze—and she remembered.

12

Tim! Where is Tim? Turning, looking up, she saw through the branches the sheer side of the hill soaring above the trees. Her legs trembling beneath her, she struggled, panic-stricken, through underbrush in that direction. She didn't have far to go. The twisted wreckage lay like a forgotten broken toy snarled among the bases of several giant trees, its main body intact.

Then she saw Tim—part of him. He, too, had been thrown from the plane, the safety belt torn loose. The lower half of his legs were hidden by the sheared-off wing.

Is he trapped under it? Has it killed him? Fearfully, Cyndi stumbled toward him. He lay on a slight incline about sixty feet above and to the side of the plane. As she passed the wreckage, she smelled gas and a terrifying thought struck her, multiplying her fears, *Fire! An explosion! Would either reach Tim? He's so close!*

When she got through the brush to Tim, she found his eyes closed, one leg twisted awkwardly, the other held captive by the tip of the wing on the downhill side. A rivulet of blood ran down his face from the gash on his forehead. Horrified at the whiteness of his face, Cyndi dropped to her knees, circled his wrist with her trembling fingers, searching for a pulse, then frantically felt at the side of his neck. Nothing . . .

Cyndi sat back on her heels, clasping her hands together, willing herself to calm down. Then again she carefully put her fingertips against his neck. She breathed a sigh of relief. "Thank you, Lord," she said quietly.

Cyndi tried with all her strength to lift the wing tip off Tim's leg, but it wouldn't budge. Breathless from the effort, she sat back on her heels beside him, untying the soft red bandana she'd been using to support her sore ankle.

She removed a small packet of facial tissues from an inside pocket of her lightweight denim jacket. Folding it into the middle of the bandana to make a thick padded area, she then placed it over the wound on his forehead and tied the scarf firmly around his head.

With a few tissues she'd kept out, she gently wiped as much blood and dirt as she could from his face, tears filling her eyes. She wished he were awake but knew he might be in great pain if he were.

Getting up and moving to his other side, she gently felt his bent leg, realizing it might be broken. Thankfully no bones were protruding. Carefully and very slowly, she moved the limb to a more normal position.

Feeling a slight chill in the air, Cyndi realized it must be late afternoon and checked her watch. The crystal was cracked but miraculously it was running.

"Five o'clock," she noted. "Unless it's very cloudy, I may have a few hours of daylight left." The patch of sky she could see between the treetops looked rather dark, but she couldn't remember what time it was when they ran into the bad weather; she supposed it must have been at least an hour since the crash.

May have been unconscious myself for a while, she thought. *It's a miracle we're alive.* She decided that since the plane hadn't already caught fire, it probably wouldn't so she went to check it out.

The smell of gas was still strong near the fuselage, but she discovered that although the gas tank hadn't ruptured, the cap must have loosened. Liquid was escaping slowly drop by drop, plopping onto a small, flat rock and sliding off to form a large spot on the sandy soil.

Carefully, fearfully, Cyndi reached out and gripped the cap, twisting it tightly; immediately the dripping stopped. Not knowing how much remained in the tank, she wasn't sure whether it would have been wiser to let it escape than to keep it there for a potential explosion, but she thought she had made the right decision.

Now I have to try to free Tim. But how? she pondered, wiping the gasoline from her hand with a bunch of green leaves. Walking back to where he lay pinned, she prayed silently, fervently, *Show me what to do, Lord. If there's something I'm capable of doing to help him, bring it to my mind.*

Tim hadn't stirred, his eyes remained closed, his face pale. Cyndi dropped to her knees beside him and put her clean hand against his cheek.

"Oh, Tim." The tears ran unheeded down her cheeks, spilling onto his blood-spattered jacket.

Suddenly in her mind's eye she could picture a storm and a tree fallen across the drive at Grandpa's home. *Of course, the fulcrum-roll! But would it work? The wing's fairly flat, not round; could I possibly move it off him? And how; what would I use?*

Cyndi scrambled to her feet, looking at the landscape of broken trees and plane wreckage, eagerly weighing the possibilities of every item her gaze touched. There were many broken branches strewn around, but they appeared to be either too small for the job or too large for her to handle.

She decided to scout around the general crash area to see if she could find something farther out. Rechecking Tim and noticing no change, she limped along, circling the crash site, carefully scrutinizing the ground and lower branches of the trees.

Joyfully she discovered her undamaged tote dangling from a branch low enough to reach with the help of a long piece of lightweight branch, and the package for Mr. Nichols in a briar patch. The wrappings were torn away but the items seemed in good condition.

Her body aching from its bruises, her weak ankle paining severely, she carried the found objects to where Tim lay silently in his partial prison. His face didn't seem quite as white as before. Cyndi hoped her eyes weren't playing tricks on her in the encroaching dimness. Kneeling beside him, she called his name several times, but received no response. Sighing deeply she got to her feet again to continue her search for implements to help remove the weight from his leg.

Cyndi moved around the area again, this time expanding her search beyond the first circle, thankfully finding two items that might be usable: a long piece of metal, which looked like the wing strut, and one of the plane's wheels, tire intact. She dragged the strut back to where Tim lay, then returned for the wheel.

It seemed extremely heavy but fortunately had settled at a slant against a large rock. She moved it to an upright position and after a struggle, rolled it between trees and scattered underbrush to the wing where she leaned it against a nearby tree.

Cyndi dropped to the ground beside Tim, her breath coming in great gasps from her effort. Daylight seemed to have faded quite a bit during her last search. She knew she'd have to work quickly if Tim was to be released before nightfall. She realized, too, that she hadn't made any type of signal pinpointing their location, if anyone guessed they were in trouble. But she doubted anything less than a fire would be noticed at dusk, and she couldn't chance even a small one, knowing it might spread. Besides, Tim's welfare must have first priority.

Cyndi sat with her hand on his shoulder studying the wing's position to determine how best to proceed. Noting one edge of the wing's far end was tight against a tree which should stabilize it, she wondered if removing debris and rocks from under the other edge would cause the wing to tip down enough to unbalance it. If so, she felt she might be able to move the tip up off Tim the way she'd moved the felled tree in Grandpa's driveway.

Glancing upward at the patch of sky visible between the treetops, she saw a dark, ominous-looking cloud passing overhead. She moved quickly, not knowing whether it was the tail of the earlier storm or another one brewing. Wishing she had a pair of heavy gloves, Cyndi rolled and shoved a basketball-size rock under the wing near the far end so the wing couldn't fall on her hands when she began moving things from beneath it.

With much grunting and pulling, she eventually cleared a space beneath the downhill edge of the wing's broad end enough, she hoped, to help the final move.

Standing on the uphill side of the wing, Cyndi then shoved a stout limb under the wing against the rock she'd placed for safety and dislodged it. With satisfaction, she observed the slight teetering of the wing. Then she rolled the wheel as near Tim as she felt she safely could, lowered it to the ground, shoved the strut under the wing tip, rested it on the tire, and sat down a minute to catch her breath.

"Lord," she prayed aloud, "I feel so weak, my legs hardly want to hold me up anymore. Please strengthen me now to do what is necessary." Then standing, she folded Mr. Nichols' new overalls over the free end of the strut to form a cushion, lay her chest across it and, planting her feet firmly, forced her weight downward in a hard lunge.

Tears filling her eyes, a heavy sob forming in her throat with the effort, Cyndi saw the wing tip rise slightly off Tim's leg. How she wished he were conscious to pull himself free.

Cyndi's entire being filled with a pleading for God's help. She shifted her weight. As she did so, the wing tip swiveled away just enough to clear Tim, the far end slipped down and the entire wing settled with a crash back to the ground, sending Cyndi sprawling.

She lay gasping, the breath knocked out of her. She wondered if she would ever breathe freely again or if she were dying. Then great sobs caught at her throat, and tears began streaming down her dirty face as breath came. Cyndi pulled her arm under her head, trying to breathe easier and soon began to calm down.

As soon as she was able, she crawled over by Tim to make sure she hadn't hurt him. As before, he didn't appear to have moved at all. The leg the wing tip had imprisoned had no bleeding or cuts, even though the pantleg was torn; she hoped the wing had balanced in such a way at the time of the crash that it didn't injure him.

Because dusk seemed to be gathering more rapidly each minute, Cyndi tried to decide what was most important to accomplish before nightfall. If clouds obscured the moon, she wouldn't be able to see at all.

Noticing again the slight chill in the air, she knew Tim would need to be protected from increasing cold during the night. She was sure she had read somewhere that an injured person could suffer from hypothermia at temperatures that wouldn't bother a well person. She wondered if it was going to get cool enough to cause problems.

I have nothing to cover him with, she thought, worry creasing her brow. Then she remembered the package for Mr. Nichols. Cyndi crawled the short space to where it lay near the strut and dragged it back near Tim to see what else was in it.

Removing Tim's shoes, she pulled a pair of heavy socks over his dress ones. Then moving quickly because of approaching darkness but carefully in case he might have unseen injuries, she struggled to put a heavy wool shirt and a pair of thick denim overalls over his other clothing, glad his dad's clothes were somewhat larger than his.

Gratified to see his forehead was no longer bleeding, she gently wrapped a T-shirt around his head for warmth and folded two others underneath for a pillow. She arranged a pair of undershorts around his neck as a scarf, pulled socks over his hands, and replaced his shoes, forcing them gently over the thick socks.

Satisfied she had done all she could for the present, Cynthia pulled the last pair of socks over her own shoes, curled up on the ground with her bent arm cradling her head and her back against Tim's arm. That way she could detect any movement should he waken. Then she prayed for no rain.

Dimness turned to deep dusk. Soon the enveloping darkness became thicker until she could no longer distinguish the plane's fuselage or the trees around them.

"Thank you, Lord, for helping me think of what to do," Cyndi said softly, tears of thanksgiving and utter weariness stealing down her cheeks.

The singing of crickets lulled her; barely noticing the soft rustlings of small night animals, she fell into a deep sleep.

13

The first faint hint of light was suggesting itself to the blackness when Cyndi awoke stiff and sore; a small cry escaped her lips when she tried to move. It was several moments before she remembered where she was. Fighting off a wave of panic, she forced herself to her knees, softly calling to Tim. Only silence answered, but his regular breathing comforted her.

Cyndi craned her neck backward, her gaze searching the filtered darkness to the space of sky between dark treetops. Two stars still dotted the darkness sharing the gap with a bright planet on its way to setting. She wondered vaguely which one it was. Venus perhaps? She curled up on the ground again, her head on her arm, hoping to sleep until daylight had really arrived.

She awoke the next time to daylight and the steady reverberating rat-a-ta-tat of a woodpecker's search for breakfast high in a cottonwood tree. Cyndi realized she was hungry and sore—most of all intensely thirsty. Where could she possibly find water? She'd seen no sign of a stream.

That would be one advantage of rain, she thought. *I might catch some to drink.* She was aware there were ways of condensing moisture from the atmosphere, but had no idea how to do it.

"A cup of hot coffee would sure be good right now," she mused, thinking of Grandpa's homey kitchen.

"Coffee. Of course, the thermos!" she remembered, getting to her feet, her legs aching and her back rebelling.

Cyndi moved stiffly toward the fuselage of the plane. Scrambling with difficulty up to the sagging door, she peered inside the compartment.

Just under the edge of a tilted seat, she saw the glint of metal from her thermos and, nearby, the ripped pharmacy bag containing the extra large bottle of aspirin Tim had bought to help relieve his dad's persistent hip pain. Certain both items were smashed, she nonetheless pulled herself into the compartment and fished them out. Although dented, the thermos was undamaged; she was glad she'd bought one with a steel rather than glass liner, happy to hear only liquid sloshing when she shook it. The paper bag was in shreds but the big plastic bottle of tablets was intact.

Sliding carefully down out of the cockpit, she took her treasures to where Tim lay.

"Tim," she called. A low moan was her answer. "Tim, wake up." But his eyelids didn't even flutter. Sighing, she sat beside him, questioning if she could safely leave him alone. She wondered if anyone knew they hadn't completed their trip. Tim hadn't said what arrangements he'd made with the tiny airport about return time.

One thing Cyndi did know was that clouds still covered at least part of the area.

Even if some people knew to search for us from the air, they probably wouldn't see us down among the trees, she thought dismally—*especially on such a dreary day.*

Cyndi unscrewed the lid cup from the thermos, poured a cup of the still-warm coffee and sat sipping it, studying ways in which she might prepare a signal pinpointing their location. She wiped the inside of the cup with half a tissue, glad she still had two extra packets in her tote, and replaced it on the thermos.

Removing her small sketch pad and pen from the tote, she began to write:

Tim, I'm going to try to reach the top of the hill behind you to place a signal. Please stay here or near the fuselage until I return. Cyndi.

Weighting the paper with the bottle of aspirin near his hand, she leaned the thermos and a packet of tissues against his side in the crook of his elbow. Selecting a slender but stout limb to use as a staff, she started out along the base of the hill.

Through underbrush, over scattered rocks, through small clearings of faded wildflowers, she walked in the early morning light. Although she knew she hadn't gone far, she was already tired and hoping the exercise would remove her stiffness, when she entered a small grove of trees. Recognizing them as willows, she thought, *There must be water nearby.* She soon located a tiny stream just beyond the edge of the trees. The water was so clear she could see the sand and tiny pebbles on the bottom. Stooping, she washed her hands and bathed her face, thankful to remove some of the oily grime—although the water was icy cold.

Cyndi saw the stream was flowing from the base of the bluff in a very shaded spot of airy ferns where the slope began a much gentler climb. She decided this was where she would make her ascent. She was fairly sure the hill's base had led her in only one direction, but without the sun she couldn't be positive.

She started to climb just to the side of a moldering tree stump covered with lichens, and a tumble of moss-covered stones that marked the stream's emergence from the slope.

Slowly she made her way upward, pausing every dozen or so steps to rest her aching ankle—still weak from her Fourth of July fall and fatigued from yesterday's events. Her binoculars swung easily from her neck; she was glad she'd left her tote behind but wished for a piece of the candy.

When Cyndi reached the hill's summit, she gathered

three stones, placed them together as a marker for her return, and made an X on each with her pen so she couldn't be mistaken about them. Lifting her binoculars, she scanned the area around her, seeing nothing but more woods. Then her gaze roved over the landscape below, finding more of the same in the distance; not a road or farm in sight.

Cyndi started out along the edge of the bluff, stopping occasionally to view both areas. Praying for guidance as she walked, she continued on, making sure to stay at the highest elevation.

Leaning against a tree to rest her ankle and use her binoculars again, Cyndi saw what appeared to be a clearing not far ahead. At the same moment she heard the distant drone of a plane's motor. With a gasp of anticipation she ran eagerly forward, reaching the cleared area just in time to see a small plane far off to the west moving away from her. Tears welled up in her eyes, but she brushed them away before they could fall.

"I have to make some sort of signal just in case they're looking for us," she decided.

Like a large meadow, the space was surrounded by forest, but near the bluff's edge the trees were a band only about a dozen deep. She went to the bluff's edge and put the binoculars to her eyes, looking straight down over the edge. Finally she caught a glimpse of red and white metal, a small portion of the wing that had trapped Tim. She couldn't see him or the fuselage, obscured by the trees and undergrowth.

The grasses around her in the plateau meadow were already beginning to dry in the lateness of the season, so Cynthia knew she couldn't safely build a signal fire.

Around and around her thoughts chased each other as her eyes searched the area again and again. How she wished a piece of the plane were up here. Its coloring would certainly be sighted if anyone passed over the area. Her gaze caught the small limb she'd been using as a staff, and an idea began to form as she walked around the area.

Cyndi worked several hours but finally had accumulated a number of large branches in the center of the open space, dragging them into position in as straight a line as she could. Panting from exertion, she stretched out in the grass to rest before continuing, seriously wondering if she would be able to do more.

Later, returning to the forested area, she collected more branches and any stones she could carry, positioning them in two lines angling out from one end of the line of larger ones, forming a giant arrow pointing toward the edge of the bluff. She dropped to the ground then, intending to rest a few minutes; instead, she fell asleep.

Cyndi woke with a feeling of warmth on her face and opened her eyes to find the rays of late-afternoon sunshine slanting through breaking cloud cover. Really wanting nothing more than to curl up and return to sleep because of her aching muscles, she forced herself to her feet and retraced her earlier path along the edge of the bluff. She stopped halfway on her route and, with the sun low at her back, raised the binoculars as before, gazing over the landscape below. She focused several times on a tiny spot above the treetops on the horizon far in the distance. Carefully she adjusted and readjusted the knob beneath her finger, focusing the glass to more definitely pinpoint what she hoped she was really seeing.

The tiny object blurred, then came into focus more distinctly. A cabin on stilts—far away to the east but definitely a fire tower.

Elated, Cyndi hurried along as best she could until she found her three X-marked stones. Digging in her heels she half slid down the long embankment, bathed her hands and face in the stream, and struck out for the wreck site.

She found Tim asleep but not where she'd left him. The thermos held down the note on which was scribbled, "Thanks." Opening the thermos she found it still half full and gratefully poured a partial cup of the still palatable liquid.

Cyndi retrieved her tote from the four-foot-high jagged tree stump where she had put it that morning and carried it to where Tim lay sleeping, propped against a tree. The socks that had been on his hands had been stuffed into ample overall pockets; the tissue packet and aspirin bottle bulged inside chest pockets of the wool shirt. She could see marks on the ground where he had struggled across the space, probably dragging one leg. A stick he'd evidently used as a cane lay beside him, and Cyndi was happy to see, even through the dirt, that some color had returned to his face.

"Tim," she said softly, sinking to her knees, hesitant about whether or not to wake him. But because she needed to talk to him, she called again, tapping his hand with her fingertips, "Tim . . . Ace."

"Ugh?" he grunted.

"It's Cyndi, Ace. Can you hear me?"

"Cyndi?" His eyelids fluttered and he peered at her through eyes only partly open.

"Yes, Tim. Cyndi. Do you remember the plane crash?"

He nodded, then shook his head slightly as though trying to clear his thoughts. He rubbed a hand across his eyes, then pulled himself to a half-sitting position.

"Are you all right, Cyndi?" he asked, deep concern in his voice.

"Yes, I'm fine. Listen, I'm sure someone will be here to get us soon, but our coffee is almost gone and I want to ask you about some water I found."

"Okay," he said, his eyes focusing on her, appearing alert.

"There's a small stream not far from here. It's quite shallow but clear as crystal and flowing from some rocks at the base of this hill," she explained. "Do you think the water is safe to drink?"

"Could be," Tim answered without hesitation. "There

are only a few known natural springs in the area with potable water, but that could be what you've found."

"I wanted to check with you first." Cyndi unscrewed the lid from the thermos. She filled the cup and handed it to him. "We'll share the rest of this; then I'll rinse the thermos and fill it with water so you'll have something to drink."

"Me?" Tim questioned. "What about you?"

"When I was on the hilltop I saw a fire tower; thought I'd hike there and get help."

"How far away do you think it is?" he asked.

Cyndi paused. "A good walk."

"How far do you estimate?" Tim persisted. "Cyndi, be honest."

"I could just make it out with my binoculars when the sun was behind me," she answered.

"That could be a very long hike in this hilly country, Cyndi," Tim said earnestly. "And if you've been hill walking today, your legs must be tired already."

Cyndi gave him a small smile, thinking, *I can't tell him all that I've done today, at least not until we've been rescued. He'd be worried and he's the one to be concerned about.*

"Anyway," Tim said, "we've probably been down a couple of hours by now, so they'll start searching and will probably find us by dark. Just sit tight."

"Okay," Cyndi said softly, wondering what he'd think if he knew they'd already been there an entire twenty-four hours.

"Well then," she said, getting to her feet, "I'll go fill the thermos and we'll have a picnic supper."

"With what?" Tim asked, not remembering.

"The things I bought. I'll be back in a little while. Anything I can do for you before I leave?"

"Yeah, any coffee left? I'd like to take some more aspirin. I hurt something fierce."

Not telling him she hadn't drunk her portion of the coffee, Cyndi emptied the small amount remaining into the cup and passed it to him, opened the aspirin bottle and shook two tablets into his upturned palm.

"Be careful," he called after her as she started off, her stick-staff and thermos in hand. Even though she was more tired than she had ever been, she forced herself to walk energetically until she was out of sight behind the surrounding trees.

Daylight was fading by the time she returned and found Tim asleep again, his back against the tree.

Cyndi had done what she could at the stream to freshen herself after filling the thermos, so while Tim slept she took items from her tote, combed her hair, slicked hand lotion on her face, smoothed some on her hands, and put on a bit of lipstick. She felt better just by trying to improve her bedraggled appearance. Then she reached over to Tim and gently shook his shoulder.

"Ace, wake up."

Tim pushed himself up, a weak grin on his face. "I'm sure useless right now; don't feel like doing anything but sleep."

"Sleep is probably the best thing for you. Do you have a pocket knife along?" she asked.

"Did have," Tim remembered, fumbling through the side opening of the overalls to his jeans pocket. "Guess it's a wonder anything stayed in my pockets. Even my wallet is still here."

"We're very lucky, Ace," Cyndi said. "We could so easily have been killed or seriously injured."

Tim nodded, and when she reached to take the folded knife, he clasped her hand. "I've been thanking God when I've been awake, but let's thank Him together, Cyndi.

"Lord, there's no way we can show our appreciation for your protection," he prayed aloud. "Help us to live the way you want us to. Maybe we can express our thanks for all our blessings this way—especially the best gift of all: salvation through Christ's death for us. Amen."

Tim continued to hold Cyndi's hand for a few moments.

"I want to thank you, too. I don't know how you managed to get me into these extra clothes, but I'm sure they'll be very welcome if we're here all night. And for whatever else you've done, Cyndi, I'm very grateful."

"It's okay, Tim," she assured. "God helped me to do whatever I needed to . . . We'll talk about it tomorrow maybe. Right now, let's have something to eat."

Cyndi removed the wheel of cheese from her tote, cut a few wedges from it, and got several wrapped hard candies from their sack.

"Guess this is it, Ace," she said with a smile. "Certainly isn't pheasant under glass or a Big Mac, but I'm thankful to have it."

"Me too, Cyndi, it actually looks good!"

While they munched on the cheese, he asked, "Have you checked the cockpit? Thought if the seats are fairly level, you might be able to get comfortable in there—use it as a bed if no one gets here soon."

Cyndi thanked him with a smile. "I was in there earlier," she said. "That's where I found the thermos and aspirin."

After they shared the candy and sips of water, Cyndi went to the detached wing for the two T-shirts still on the ground where she'd folded them under Tim's head the previous night. Gathering leaves from sheared-off branches, she stuffed them into the shirts, forming a makeshift pillow for each of them.

They talked awhile as darkness closed in; then Cyndi handed him a pillow and headed for the downed plane.

"Night, Ace," she said. "Call if you need me."

"Good-night, Cyndi," he answered. "Hope you sleep well. Thanks again for your help." Then so softly she almost didn't hear it, "God bless you, honey."

Cyndi crawled up into the cockpit area with her tote, wondering if she could possibly get comfortable enough to sleep. Ace evidently hadn't noticed in his lethargic condition the crazy slant at which the fuselage had hit the ground. After much scooting around, she finally decided the most logical position would be sitting on the angled floor and leaning against the seat cushion, which would be a backrest of sorts. Trying to get situated among the control stick and pedals, she felt something shift under her knee.

Groping with her hand, she pulled out a pocket-size metal box. Because darkness had fallen, she decided to wait until morning to check its contents, wiped it off on her jeans, and shoved it in the outside pouch of her tote.

With the makeshift pillow under her head, the seat back forming a canopy over her head and the tote braced to keep her from sliding, Cyndi fell asleep while praying for God's care through another night at the crash site.

14

Cyndi awoke, feeling stiff but mentally alert when daylight was just beginning to seep into the area beneath the dense growth of trees. Uncurling her legs she pushed herself through the door opening and slid to the ground with her tote. After straightening her hair and clothes, she went to Tim and woke him.

"Tim, drink all the water you want. I'm going to refill the thermos. Do you need aspirin?"

He nodded. Pulling himself to a sitting position, he drank two cups of water with the pills she handed him. Cyndi drank some, then moistened a tissue in the remainder so he could freshen his face. "Thanks, Cyndi," he said with a weak smile.

"I'll be back in a little while," she said. Taking the thermos she made her way to the stream, washed a little in the clear, cold water, and drank her fill after refilling the thermos for Tim.

Wearily she got to her feet. When she returned, Tim was sleeping again. Then she remembered the small metal box she'd discovered in the plane. Cyndi took it from her tote and opened it. Inside was a tiny compass on a chain, a roll of thin wire, and a vial of matches. Slipping the compass chain around her neck, she put the box in her tote.

Cyndi cut a wedge of cheese, ate it, and put another in her pocket. Slipping a handful of wrapped candies in another pocket, she put some in one of Tim's. She was placing the thermos and the wrapped cheese beside him on a mat of moss when she heard the rustling in the underbrush followed by a strange buzzing. Although Cyndi didn't recognize its source, instantly a strange prickling at the back of her neck alerted her as she saw something near Tim's head in a patch of dry leaves.

"Tim, a rattlesnake!" she screamed, shaking him awake.

He stared groggily at her. "What?"

"The snake! Right there!" she gasped, pointing.

"Oh, Cyndi," Tim said, chuckling even in his weakness, yet looking a bit exasperated. "Don't you remember the day by the stream? That's just a fox snake, a great rattler-mimic."

Chagrined, she said, "I'm sorry for startling you like that, Ace. I thought the thing was going to strike you. I still can't tell one snake from another; to me they're all creepy, slithery things.

"But since you're awake, I want you to know I'm starting out for the fire tower. I'll leave a note in the cockpit."

Tim nodded. "Be careful, Cyndi." Then grinning, he said, "You can always distinguish a poisonous snake by its eyes; they have slit-shape pupils like a cat's."

"Okay," she said, knowing she'd never want to get close enough to check.

She looked at her watch—six a.m. Then sitting on a nearby stump, she took her sketchpad and pen from her pocket, quickly writing two notes:

> *Left crash site approximately six a.m. heading east; hoping to reach sighted fire tower and get assistance for wounded pilot. Cynthia Carlson*

She put one of the notes in the plane, weighting the other with the thermos beside Tim.

Then quickly writing a copy of them, she added: *Downed plane and injured pilot marked by brush arrow in forest plateau clearing.* This one she slipped in her pocket.

Just in case I can't find anyone before I collapse, she thought morbidly.

I probably should climb up to the clearing and get a definite directional fix on the tower now that I have a compass, Cyndi thought as she waved goodbye to Tim. *But it would take time and too much of my energy; think I'll just start in the general direction and take a chance on hitting a road or path to someone's home or camp area.*

She found the hike in the misty light of early morning beneath the crowding trees pleasant, the first hour not especially difficult as she covered level land with only moderate underbrush.

Cyndi kept an almost constant check on the compass, moving quickly along, glad for the occasional company of singing birds and various little animals moving through their forest home. She had stopped a moment to catch her breath when a small white-faced gray fox crossed her path, stopping to stare warily at her a moment before disappearing among the trees.

The first I've ever seen except in pictures, she realized, wishing she had time to get her pad from her pocket and quickly sketch him. But concern for Tim pushed her on.

She checked the compass again, wishing she were wearing hiking shoes instead of lightweight sneakers. The going was getting rougher now, although it was a fine day of clear blue skies and warm breezes. Sunshine filtering through the trees highlighted occasional clearings bright with lingering wildflowers.

By noon Cyndi was very tired; the hills were causing extra strain on her weak ankle, which was hurting a lot now. Sitting on a fallen tree, she ate part of the wedge of cheese, longing for a cool drink. Unwrapping a piece of candy, she sucked on it, which helped a little. She noticed a grassy, mossy area beneath a group of full-foliaged, low-branched trees when she bent to massage her ankle and decided to stretch out there a few minutes to ease her sore leg.

Cyndi rolled over, stretched, yawned, and looked at her watch. Startled she sat up, checking it again.

I couldn't have slept almost five hours! She got to her feet, dismayed to know she had slept through the afternoon.

Hurrying ahead to a clearing where she could view the sky, she saw that the sun was most certainly low in the west. Because another hill was ahead on her eastern course, she hiked quickly, hoping to see the fire tower from its crest.

Cyndi located the tower easily, about two miles to the north. She was glad to know she'd judged the original direction accurately and hadn't wasted time covering the wrong ground. Hoping the way wouldn't be as difficult as it had been in the morning, so she could reach the tower before dark, she hurried on. Most of all, she hoped someone would be there when she arrived.

When she came to a path angling off a bit from her plotted course, she decided to follow it, discovering after a while a crudely made sign carved into a tree-slab mounted on a post at the side of the path: *Walnut Ridge, Fire Tower Number Seven, 1 mile.*

"That's Tim's tower!" Cyndi exclaimed excitedly. "At least I can phone someone from there." She quickened her pace, realizing she was close to help. Diminishing daylight beneath the dense growth of trees meant the sun would soon be setting, and she didn't want Tim alone once night fell—he might still be feeling disoriented. She wondered as she hurried along what the day had been like for him and hoped his injuries weren't causing complications or unbearable pain.

She followed the narrow, overgrown path, finally reaching the clearing where the tower's base was already in semidarkness. The four metal legs soaring above the treetops held the cabin where the last lingering rays of sunlight flashed on its western windows.

Cyndi sat a minute on the bottom step regaining her breath for the 123-stair climb. But her concern for Tim caused her to keep on.

When she pushed up through the trapdoor, she was dumbfounded—the cabin was empty! Absolutely everything was gone except the chair and the broom standing in its usual corner. Cyndi gazed around the cabin's interior, unable to believe her eyes. The alidade and its cabinet were no longer there, nor the iron box that held the radio, nor the phone.

The phone! Cyndi's concern rose. *How can I get help for Tim without a phone or radio? I have no idea how to reach his home or whether there's another nearby . . .*

Pulling the chair to one of the windows, she sat down with a sigh, putting the binoculars to her eyes and scanning the surrounding area. Nothing but forest until she spotted another tower to the south.

Must be Bluebird, she concluded. *If only I had some way to signal.* Then remembering her compact-mirror and the shiny metal box in her tote, she used first one then the other to flash an *S.O.S.* using the last of the sun's rays. But she received no answering flash.

Either the angle is wrong or that tower may be empty, too, she thought. *The change-over to helicopter reconnaissance may have already begun. The phase-out of Ace's tower could be the reason he felt able to be away almost a month; strange he didn't mention it.*

Discouraged, Cyndi stood to check in other directions. Through a window at the opposite side of the cabin, she saw among the trees what appeared to be a stone wall, barely discernible in the twilight.

"Must be the old mill," she mused, remembering the cool water swirling around her ankles, wishing she had a drink; she was so thirsty.

"Sure hope the water I left with Ace was safe to drink," she said aloud, still scanning the area with her binoculars. Noticing nothing helpful except a few less densely forested areas that might be farms, she left the cabin and wearily descended the long flight of stairs.

Because of the overgrown condition of the path she'd followed to reach the tower, she was sure it wasn't Tim's usual route. She paused on the bottom step, her gaze searching the rim of the clearing. Seeing an opening in the trees, she started forward then stopped, remaining absolutely still a moment to watch three forms move from just beyond the trees. Silently, gracefully, three beautiful brown deer stepped through soft, golden twilight, then glided across the clearing before disappearing again among the trees.

Glad she hadn't frightened them, Cyndi hurried across to what she hoped was a path or drive that would lead her to a traveled road. Just before she reached it, she sighted a most welcome item.

A hand pump! Cyndi thought delightedly. *Just like the one in Grandpa's backyard . . . hope it's primed.* Hurrying over to it, she put her tote on the ground, grasped the handle, and began pumping vigorously. She was soon rewarded with gushing water, splashing on a rock placed to prevent erosion.

Cyndi washed her hands, then drank some water by bending over, her hand cupped around the spout as Grandpa had shown her years before. Concern for Tim was deepening as she realized daylight was fast disappearing. *I've got to get help for him soon,* she thought, wiping her hands on her jeans. Slipping her tote strap over her shoulder, she crossed a small parking area to a gravel road. She turned in the direction of what she believed was the mill, hoping the road there would be well traveled and that this one connected with it.

Except for choruses of crickets and the light crunch of her sneakers on gravel, the forest was silent around her. Cyndi munched on part of the wedge of cheese still left in her pocket, wishing she'd had something in which to carry water from the pump.

Dusk was gathering more heavily now and stars began dotting the darkening sky. Cyndi stopped where the gravel road crossed a blacktop, wondering whether to go right or left. She had no idea whether the road she'd been on had taken her in a straight line or not, and she hadn't bothered to check the compass since leaving the tower because she couldn't read the dial in the twilight.

She unwrapped a piece of candy—even the crackle of the cellophane sounded loud in the quiet evening. As she hesitated, another sound, distinctive and easily distinguishable, came to her through the clear air: the slamming of a car door.

There's someone within walking distance for sure, Cyndi thought. *Wish I knew exactly where. If I wasn't hearing an echo, it's somewhere to the right.* She started down the blacktop, hoping to find the source of that noise.

As she jogged unevenly along, she glanced up at the expanse of star-studded darkness and gasped at the striking beauty of a meteor suddenly streaking across the sky.

On and on she went, feeling she'd been on this road a long time, wondering if she had missed a driveway or lane in the dusk. Darkness was settling deeper, and Cyndi began to feel a bit frightened.

She paused a moment to listen, straining her ears to hear something—anything—that would let her know she was nearing an occupied area.

Suddenly light began to dispel the darkness as the moon rose above the forest, its full roundness bathing the area in moonlight.

The harvest moon, Cyndi thought. *What a welcome sight. Clouds must have covered it last night.* In a few moments Cyndi could easily see the road. She noted that she had been passing fields, and could distinguish fence posts and a field of corn.

Off to the left she thought she saw a light between the trees and debated cutting across the fields and woods to reach it. When it disappeared after a few minutes, she decided to continue along the blacktop until she found a road or lane leading in that general direction. Although she had an idea of where she was, nothing really looked familiar.

Cyndi's concern for Tim kept mounting. *This will be another night spent outdoors with his injuries and without ample food or water,* she frowned. Praying silently for him, she hurried along, being careful not to stumble. *I wonder if he'll be able to pull himself up into the cockpit if it rains?*

Ahead on her left she saw an opening in the dilapidated

fence. Reaching the spot, she found a lane.

It looks so overgrown. Cyndi hesitated about following it, fearful of finding only deserted buildings and wasting time. But the light appeared again, helping her decide, so she followed the lane, which consisted of two dirt paths separated by tall grass and weeds.

After going a short way, certain she heard voices in the distance, Cyndi broke into a limping jog. A minute more and the voices became discernible. Two men were talking loudly as though they were arguing. Again she saw the lights, probably flashlights, near a sagging barn.

Cyndi didn't know what to do. She was fearful of approaching strange men who seemed ready for a fight, but thoughts of Tim alone and suffering spurred her on. She was about to call out when another light appeared. Separated from the others by a wide space, it was shaped like a window.

Must be a house. I'll check there. That's where the phone would be anyway, she decided, thankful she might not have to face the men.

Even with just the moon for light, Cyndi could tell that the house, like the barn, had seen better days. She stumbled on a broken step, sending a metal pail clattering. A child inside the house began to whimper, then cry in earnest.

Cyndi sidestepped missing floorboards on the porch, noticing the sagging railing, the cardboard patch in the window. Through the dingy pane of another window beside the door, she saw an old-fashioned oil lamp on the table, a worn-looking woman in a rocking chair holding the sobbing child.

They may not even have a phone, Cyndi reflected unhappily. She heard a car door slam in the direction of the barn and a motor start. She reached out a hand to knock. As the sound of the motor receded down the lane, suddenly she heard a step behind her.

"What'd ya want?"

Startled, Cyndi turned. Because the moon was behind him, she couldn't see the features of the man mounting the steps. He reached across the narrow porch and grabbed her arm, pulling her toward the lighted window, turning her so he could see her face. The heavy smell of liquor was strong on him.

"You!" he said, his voice hard as they recognized each other. "Thought I warned you last time! What ya always snoopin' 'round for? Now what'll I do with ya?"

"I wanted—" Cyndi started, but not waiting for an answer, he pushed the door open, shoving her through ahead of him.

The woman stared at them, alarm and fear on her face, clasping the suddenly shrieking youngster against her breast.

"Shut that kid up!" the man snarled. "An ya ain't seen no one, understand?"

The woman nodded mutely, shushing the youngster, smoothing the dark curls as Cyndi was propelled roughly across the bare floor and through another door. Pushing her inside, he slammed the door shut; she heard a key turn in the lock.

15

Picking herself up from the splintery floor, Cyndi wrinkled her nose as she sniffed the air in the room; not only was it stale, it had a strange acrid smell. "Must have kept chickens in here at one time," she mused.

Soon the child's crying changed to subdued sobs and Cyndi heard muffled voices: the woman's low and pleading; the man's harsh, demanding. Cyndi wanted very much to call out, to explain why she was here and ask that the authorities be notified so Tim could be brought home.

She tapped on the door. "Sir," she called, "please let me explain. I need to phone—"

"Shut up in there!" he shouted.

"But my friend needs help," she persisted.

"You'll be the one needin' help!"

Peering through the darkness around her, Cyndi could barely discern a horizontal slit of light on the opposite side of the room. Moving carefully so she wouldn't fall over anything, she discovered the slit was moonlight shining beyond a crack between planks of a boarded-up window. Since the boards were on the outside, she felt for a lock joining the window's sections. Sliding the latch, she tried without success to push the bottom part up.

"Must be nailed shut or stuck from layers of old paint," Cyndi said softly. "Now what?"

Praying silently, fervently for help, she felt her way around the edges of the dark room and found another immoveable window, a few cardboard boxes, and beyond the other edge of the door next to a crate, a small rocking chair. Thankfully she sank into it, glad for a place to rest, weary from the day's events, her thoughts muddled from this latest disappointment. For some time she rethought her situation, praying for guidance.

I was so sure I'd finally reached help for Tim. What if no one is searching and I can't get away from here soon? What will happen to him?

After a time Cyndi noticed that the house was quiet; she could hear crickets singing their nighttime melodies. Getting up, she felt her way to the windows, trying again to force them open, but with no success. Then, as she turned in despair from the second one, her hand brushed across the sash and touched cardboard. Cyndi realized this window must be patched just like the one on the porch.

That means part of the glass is missing—maybe enough for me to crawl through if I can also remove the outside boards, she thought excitedly as she moved her hands back to the window, rechecking the possible opening size.

The turning of the key in the lock sounded loud to Cyndi's ears in the silent house. Fear gripped her as she turned to face the door. It opened slowly, illuminating the figure of a woman against the murky light of the oil lamp.

Relieved, Cyndi heard her whisper, "You all right, young lady?"

"Yes, I'm okay," she answered quietly.

"I'm Sally," the woman said softly. "I brought you something to eat." Cyndi heard the rustle of a paper sack as Sally put it on the crate and added, "Be right back. I'm going to the kitchen to get some hot coffee; haven't any tea, hope that's okay."

"Coffee's fine; and thank you, Sally. But what about your husband, where is he?"

"Fell asleep . . . been drinking heavy so probably won't

wake till late morning. I'm sorry 'bout the way he treated you." Sally disappeared out the door and around a corner.

Cyndi sat in the rocker, thankful at the sudden turn of affairs. Opening the sack, she put the wrapped sandwich and an apple on her lap.

Sally returned, walking carefully, silently. She put two mugs on the crate and sat beside them.

"You go ahead and eat," she said softly. "I'll have coffee with you. Forgot to ask you, but put milk in it; don't have no sugar."

"It'll be fine, Sally. I'm so thirsty and hungry." Cyndi answered. "I've been walking more than half the day. Do you have a phone?"

"No, not much of anything here; place is awful run down," Sally said. "We're only supposed to be here for the summer. Bert hoped to make enough on the crop for us to rent a decent place for the winter, but Potter's trying to cheat him, he says—"

Sally stopped. "I'm sorry, here I'm pouring out my troubles and haven't even asked your name and why you came here."

"I'm Cyndi Carlson. There was a plane crash and my friend is injured. I must get help . . . Does a neighbor have a phone?"

"A plane crash! You were in a crash? Are you hurt?" Sally was crouching before Cyndi, her hands on Cyndi's arms; in the faint light from the lamp in the next room, Cyndi saw the deep concern on the other woman's face.

"I'm okay, just tired mostly. But a phone; do you have a neighbor nearby?" Cyndi urged.

"Don't know anyone . . . Bert makes me stay close to the house. He does the grocery shopping and such. You mustn't hate Bert for this; it's the drink mainly. He was a good man till several years ago when he got to working for Potter." Sally's voice was tense, tired. Cyndi felt sorry for her.

"Even little Samantha is afraid of him most times 'cause he gets angry so easily and hollers so; hits us sometimes."

"Sally, you've unlocked this door. You'll let me leave while your husband's asleep, won't you?"

Fear tinged Sally's voice. "I couldn't do that, Cyndi," she said, jumping up to block the doorway. "I'd like to, honest. I know this isn't right, but he might . . . I don't know what he might do to me, even little Samantha, much as he loves her. I don't know if I could stop you but I'd have to try, 'cause he gets real violent—worse, much worse than tonight."

Cyndi sat silently for a few moments, then said calmly, "I don't want to cause you any harm, Sally, but I have to think about my friend, too. If I can get away, making it look as though I'd escaped without anyone's help, would you interfere?"

Slowly Sally came back to sit on the crate. "No," she said. "But how could you do that without him knowing? He'd blame me for sure."

Quietly Cyndi explained her plan of escape through the damaged window.

"But the windows are boarded up on the outside," Sally said.

"Do you have something I could loosen the window with and remove the boards?" Cyndi asked. "Some sort of prying tool and maybe a putty-knife or something similar to cut the paint or glue that's been put around the sash?"

"Might be tools in the old barn, but I wouldn't dare get them for you even if I could find them. He'd know I was the only who one could have helped you. Bert usually sleeps long and real sound near morning when he drinks like tonight, but if he woke up and caught me . . ." After a pause she added, "Could get you a kitchen knife, though, if it'd be any help."

"I'll give it a try," Cyndi said. "Please hurry."

After Sally left the room, Cyndi was tempted to just run across the other room, out the front door, and into the night.

It was the sensible thing to do; she knew she was crazy not to. Yet something held her back. She decided to at least try to cooperate with Sally. Maybe she could get away without implicating the woman.

By then Sally was back with a flashlight and a plate on which was a slice of buttered bread, a dab of jelly, a knife, and a heavy, medium-sized spoon. She put the spoon in Cyndi's cup, picked up her own, and placed the flashlight on the crate by the dishes. "He won't fault me for bringing you something to eat, Cyndi." She turned to go.

"Wait, Sally," Cyndi whispered, bending to get her tote from the floor. Reaching inside, she removed the tiny New Testament she'd always carried in one of its inside pockets, the package of tea and the candies. Slipping them in the pocket of Sally's apron, Cyndi hugged her, whispering, "For you and Samantha. I'll be praying for you."

Sally shyly hugged her back. "Please wait a few hours till Bert's real sound asleep for sure before you do anything, so there's little chance of waking him."

After Sally had locked the door behind her, Cyndi turned the flashlight on. The room was much as she'd determined earlier with one window intact and boarded on the outside. Moonlight showed through slits between the boards.

When she turned the light on the other window located near the corner of the room, she found most of the bottom pane covered with tacked-on cardboard.

Using the spoon's bowl tip, Cyndi patiently pulled the large tacks. Removing the cardboard, she found only a corner of the pane remaining. Carefully, slowly she felt around the sash, making sure there were no glass fragments that would cut her when she crawled through.

Pausing in her work, she listened intently to a sound she'd heard a few moments before and now again. *Snoring,* she realized. *Sally's husband is on the other side of this wall. Their bedroom must open off the front as this one does. How am I going to force the planks off the window without waking him?*

Deciding she would have to just take it one step at a time, beginning with waiting as Sally had suggested, Cyndi found her way to the rocker. She realized after a time that she must have dozed, because she didn't even hear crickets now. She got the knife from the crate, glad the flatware seemed made from sturdy old steel rather than a silver mixture.

Reaching through the opening of the broken window, she pushed gently on one of the center boards covering the window's lower half, finding it strong but a trifle springy at one end. The beam of the flashlight revealed a crack between the board and the outside window frame. Cyndi slipped the knife blade into the crack, pulled it up and down until she located the nails, then tried using it as a prying tool.

The board moved outward just a bit, but enough to also insert the thickness of the spoon handle. Leaving the implements inserted there, Cyndi stooped, removed her sneakers and socks, then folded the socks into pads to keep from injuring her hands while prying the ends of the board loose. Finally the piece of wood was hanging by just one end; when she pried the last nail the rest of the way out, the board fell before she could grab it and dropped with a clatter on something metal below.

Cautiously she listened, her ear almost against the wall. Silence. *Did Bert wake up?* she wondered. Frantically trying to think what to do if that happened and he came to check on her, Cyndi held her breath, listening. Then the snoring began again.

"Thank you, Lord," Cyndi whispered, resolving to be more careful. Not sure she could keep the other boards from falling as she removed the nails, she considered her options and remembered the roll of thin wire in the metal box that had held the compass. She got it out, wondering if it would be strong enough for what she was considering.

Returning to the window, Cyndi proceeded to pry off the

bottom board, certain the opening would be big enough for her to crawl through. When it was partly loosened, she unrolled the wire, ran it behind her waist, the other end around the board so it might shift a bit but not fall when the nails were all pried loose. She twisted the wire's ends firmly, loosened the last nails, and maneuvered the board inside, standing it against the wall. Then she unfastened the wire from her waist.

After putting the knife and spoon beside the board, hoping to make it clear to Bert she'd escaped by her own efforts, she quickly replaced her socks and sneakers.

Shielding the beam as much as possible, she shined the flashlight to the ground below the window, discovering an old overturned tub. *As long as the noise of the board hitting it didn't wake Sally's husband, I'm glad it's there,* she thought. *I can use it as a step when I go out.*

As she prepared to crawl out, Cyndi faced a dilemma. Knowing the flashlight would be useful but aware its disappearance could cause trouble for Sally and her child, she decided to take it and return it as soon as possible.

Careful to avoid the sharp wedge of glass in the corner, Cyndi slid a leg over the sill, glad the windows in the old house were low to the ground. Cautiously she felt for the upturned tub, hoping it wasn't badly rusted and would hold her weight. Ducking her head and inching her body through the opening, she breathed a sigh of relief as her foot found the tub firm beneath her foot.

When she was safely on the ground, Cyndi headed straight for the seclusion of the barn's shadows to get her bearings.

The moon was setting, with dawn already on the other horizon. Cyndi knew she must get away as quickly as possible, not only for her and Sally's safety but to find a phone.

Flicking the flashlight on only briefly to get the lay of the land, she picked her way across the littered yard. Stopping in deep shadow at the end of the barn, Cyndi noticed again the odor of a chicken coop, reminding her of Grandpa's chickens, which had been without attention for two days. She was sure the ample waterer would still be partly filled but wondered if the chickens had been able to get along on insects and weeds along the edge of their run. Milk wasn't due to be delivered until this morning; at least she didn't have to be concerned about it souring. She inwardly laughed at herself for even thinking about sour milk at a time like this.

Cyndi slipped inside the barn and swept the light's beam around inside, amazed at the many bundles of foliage hanging from walls and rough racks. They reminded her of herbs from her grandmother's garden, drying in the barn with bunches of wildflowers for sachets and holiday arrangements.

Someone must have a flourishing business with gift shops, she thought, not noticing in her brief glance that the plants were all of one species.

Able to faintly distinguish the fence that marked the lane, Cyndi got her bearings and struck out diagonally across the wide field to save time and avoid being seen from the house. When she reached the far edge, she climbed a section of broken fence and was soon on the blacktop well beyond Bert's lane.

As she jogged along the edge of the road, she realized that in her haste she'd left her tote behind.

"Like a pack rat, I took a flashlight and left my tote," she chided herself softly. "Maybe I can secretly visit Sally soon and make an exchange."

Dawn was definitely breaking now, allowing Cyndi to see her surroundings. She was jogging past another neglected meadow-like field when she stopped, walked closer to the edge, and shined her light on the overgrown area. Definite vehicle tracks led through the grassy weeds back along a fence row to a woods in the distance—the area where Bert had accosted her the first time.

Jogging along the road again, Cyndi noticed a moving

light off to the right, a vehicle approaching along the next crossroad. She sprinted ahead, trying to reach there by the time it did.

Flicking the flashlight on she pointed in that direction, turning it on and off in S.O.S. sequence as she ran.

The pickup truck reached the crossroads before she did but turned in her direction. It slowed as it approached, then stopped beside her. The face of the man who leaned out the window seemed vaguely familiar.

"Well, Miss Carlson! I'll be switched. What ya'll doin' out here joggin' along so early?"

Gasping for breath, Cyndi couldn't answer immediately, so he continued, "Was on my way to deliver milk to you and the store in town. How 'bout climbin' in and I'll just drop you off with the milk."

"Thanks, Mr. Darby." Cyndi dropped the flashlight in her pocket as she walked around the truck to get in on the passenger side. He made a U-turn and as soon as she caught her breath, Cyndi explained the incidents of the past few days, omitting the run-in with Bert.

"Well, what d'ya know! The wife and I heard a missing plane mentioned on the news day before yesterday. Last night they said it still hadn't been found. Sure never dreamed 'twas you." Mr. Darby shook his head, clucking his tongue. "An' that poor young man still out there alone. He's a good boy, Nichols' son is. Think I should take you straight into town to the police station so you can tell them?"

"I'll call from home first if you don't mind waiting; then if necessary I'll ride in with you."

Grandpa's house was a most welcome sight to Cyndi. While Mr. Darby put the milk in the refrigerator for her, Cyndi dialed the Milltown police.

Briefly explaining who she was and Tim's condition as far as she knew, she added, "The wreckage is located at the base of large trees just below the rock face of a large hill, north of a small natural spring. It's about an eight-hour walk mostly west of the Walnut Ridge fire tower. There's an open meadow on the hill's summit. I made an arrow out of tree brush."

Cyndi listened a moment, then, "Yes, they could climb down from a spot where there are three stones placed together with X's marked on them, but getting a stretcher back up might be rather difficult . . . What? . . . Turn left when you reach the bottom; you'll find a small stream. It's a five- or ten-minute walk to the site. His name is Tim Nichols."

Cyndi replaced the receiver and turned to Mr. Darby who stood waiting in the dining room doorway, "I don't have to go to the station. They hadn't found the wreckage yet because we were evidently far off the expected course for the trip we were on."

"I sure am glad I saw you, Miss Carlson," Mr. Darby said. "There anything I can do for you before I go on?"

Wearily Cyndi tried to think.

"Grandpa's chickens . . . I haven't been able to tend to them for two days. Would you please water them? There's feed in the barn, if you don't mind doing that, too."

"Surely glad to do it. Don't you worry none 'bout 'em. Many's the favor your grandpa's done for me over the years. You try to get some rest. They'll find Ace. He's a strong fellow; he'll be fine."

Cyndi smiled her thanks as Mr. Darby closed the kitchen door behind him. Then she lifted the receiver and dialed the Nichols' number, knowing Tim's dad must be very worried.

When she had finished her conversation with him, Cyndi took a shower, had a quick breakfast of toast and milk, then went upstairs. After praying again for Tim, she crawled into bed, lying, thinking, *I don't think bed has ever felt so wonderful!*

She was wakened by the persistent ringing of the phone, which continued until she had sleepily descended the stairs and answered it.

"Cyndi! This is Jennifer. I just heard the good news on

the radio here at the office. Everyone's been frantic!"

"Did they find Tim?"

"They were telling about your return and that searchers had been sent out again when an announcer broke in with a special report, saying the wreckage had been located easily because of your arrow and other directions," Jennifer said.

"But what about Tim? Is he all right?" Cyndi asked anxiously.

"The report said he was being taken by helicopter to the hospital in Halesburg and seemed to be in fairly good condition," Jennifer answered.

"I'm so thankful," Cyndi said. "I was so worried."

"I can imagine," Jennifer agreed. "We were concerned about both of you when Mr. Nichols phoned the pastor to say you were missing. Everyone at the church was praying."

"Thank you for telling me that, Jen. Please let them know how very much I appreciate their prayers for us."

"I will, Cyndi . . . I'll phone tomorrow about our shopping date. Try to relax now. Anything I can do for you in the meantime?"

"No thanks, Jen; everything's taken care of," Cyndi answered. When Jennifer had hung up, Cyndi said to herself, "Almost everything," as she dialed Mr. Nichols' number to give him the welcome news in case he hadn't heard the newscast or been notified. Then she called the Halesburg Hospital to get a report on Tim, relieved to find he was doing well.

After the calls, she dressed and went to the tower, convinced that Mr. Nichols would keep her up-to-date on reports from the hospital during the next several days.

Cyndi and Jennifer agreed the next day to shop in Halesburg on Saturday so they could also visit Tim. They decided, too, that Jennifer would come to Cyndi's Friday for supper and spend the night so they could leave early the next morning.

Jennifer was delayed Friday and dusk had already fallen

by the time Cyndi heard a car approaching. Sure it was her friend, she hurriedly slipped the pan of biscuits into the oven and set the coffeepot over a flame before heading through the dining room toward the front door.

Entering the living room, she saw a face peering through a window at the side of the room. Terrified eyes looked into hers and then the face disappeared as the car turned into the drive.

16

Cynthia had flung the door open, raced along the lighted porch, and leaned over the railing looking down the side of the house by the time Jennifer had stopped her car.

"That's an exuberant greeting," Jennifer laughed, stepping out. "What on earth are you looking for?"

Glancing carefully around the yard obscured by twilight, Cyndi descended the steps. "Someone was looking in the window . . . Evidently ran away when you arrived."

"Sounds scary." Jennifer looked around, too. "Any idea who it was?"

"No," Cyndi answered as they climbed the porch steps and she held the door for her friend. "But it sure spooked me."

"Are your other doors locked?" Jennifer asked, setting her overnight bag on the floor.

Cyndi nodded, turning to lock the one they'd just entered. "I've been leaving the windows locked except in the kitchen because I like to have them open when I'm there."

It suddenly dawned on her that someone could break in there. She rushed to the kitchen, shutting and locking the windows and drawing the shades.

"I feel kind of silly, but it would be foolish to leave them, I suppose, with someone snooping around," she told Jennifer.

They put dinner on the table and, while eating, discussed the Peeping Tom. After a while, Cyndi said, "Actually, Jen, thinking about it, I believe the face appeared more like a woman's than a man's, though I couldn't be sure in the dusk. Besides, I only saw it for a second before it disappeared. It sure seems strange . . ."

"Frightening is more like it," Jennifer stated, her red hair bouncing against her shoulders as she stood to help clear the table before dessert.

Tap-Tap-Tap. Both girls froze in their tracks, staring at each other as the tapping on the window sounded again.

Cyndi flipped the light switch off, stepped across the darkened room to the window and slowly raised the shade. The moon was rising, its illumination backlighting the figure at the window: a woman holding a child.

"It's Sally, Miss Carlson . . . Sally and my little Samantha."

"My goodness!" Cyndi exclaimed. "Come around to the door." She motioned the direction and went to unlock it, snapping on the light switch. Stepping onto the screened-in porch, she called, "Over here, Sally!"

Cyndi led her into the kitchen, then stopped in dismay.

"Oh, Sally, did Bert do that to you?"

Sally nodded, tears welling in her blackened eyes at the concern in Cyndi's voice.

"Here, sit down." Jennifer quickly pulled out a chair.

Sally did so, Cyndi's tote swinging by its strap from her shoulder, little Samantha clutching her mother's neck, staring uncertainly at the two young women. The welt on the child's cheek was as obvious as the mother's bruised eyes.

"What happened?" Cyndi asked, slipping the tote off Sally while Jennifer put butter and jam on a biscuit, offering it to Samantha.

"Bert was awful mad when he woke up the other morning and found you gone. He was feeling rotten anyway from the drink of the night before."

"Is that when he hit you?"

Sally shook her head. "He just raved some. When he settled down, he said you probably hadn't seen anything anyway so good riddance."

"Seen anything?" Cyndi asked, perplexed.

"Potter's got some kind of deal going with him, and I'm getting more and more scared that it's not legal," Sally explained.

"I see . . ." Cyndi knew she really didn't understand what was going on. "Have you and Samantha had supper?" she asked, smiling at the little girl.

Sally shook her head again.

"Well then, I'll reheat the chili and pour milk for Samantha while Jen gets a cushion to make this chair high enough."

Turning to the stove, Cyndi added, "Oh, I'm sorry. Sally, this is my friend, Jennifer Martin; Jen, this is Sally." The introduction was acknowledged with smiles; then Jennifer went for the cushion, prepared the chair for the little girl, and helped her get seated next to her mother.

While the two ate, Sally said, "I didn't mean to be a bother. You were kind to me after my Bert did you wrong, and I just wanted to return your bag."

"How did you ever find me?" Cyndi asked.

"You had a kind of map in your bag showing the roads leading to town with a few landmarks like the fire tower and a spot marked '*Grandpa's house.*' There're good signs at all the crossroads so 'twasn't any trouble 'cept the walking."

"Grandpa sketched the surrounding areas for me when I first came so I could find my way around," Cyndi explained.

"I figured if you weren't here, I'd just leave the bag on the porch," Sally continued. "We were out of most food this morning, so I asked Bert if I could go into town for groceries this time . . . Thought I'd stop by here on the way if I could find your place. But before Bert could think about it, Potter came by and they had a terrible row out at the barn, and when Bert came in he was acting fierce.

"Drank and talked real rough the next couple hours,

smoking those funny cigarettes he's been using lately, too. When I saw he was getting drowsy, I asked him if I could have the keys to the truck." Sally stopped, her mouth twisting, trying not to cry. "Suddenly he was wide awake. He jumped up and hit me a couple times. Little Samantha started screaming, she was so scared, an' he smacked her too." Sally couldn't stop the tears now. "He's only been this way lately. He loves us, I know he does. It's like he's been pushed to the limit worryin' about Potter. Then when he drinks . . ." her voice trailed off.

Cyndi refilled Sally's coffee cup and removed the empty chili bowls, trying at the same time to divert Samantha, whose little face was puckering with concern at her mother's tears and strained voice.

"Where is your husband now?" Jennifer asked, slicing an extra peach for the visitors' shortcake.

"He took off in the truck. Don't know if he's comin' back. I was afraid to leave and afraid to stay, too. So I decided to see if I could find you. I read some of the New Testament yesterday an' I got some questions."

After they'd all agreed Sally would spend the night there, Cyndi and Sally bathed a sleepy Samantha, then put her to bed in the upstairs room next to Cyndi's, tucking the old stuffed bear from the rocking chair beside her. Before her eyes drooped shut, the little girl gave Cyndi a sweet smile, snuggling her curly head against the old bear's tummy.

How could a man hit such an innocent little one? Cyndi wondered, knowing at the same time that according to the news, it happens over and over again, in all kinds of families. Before turning off the bedroom light, she snapped on a small nightlight, leaving a soft, cheery glow around the sleepy child so she wouldn't be frightened if she woke up before her mother came to bed.

Cyndi and Sally tiptoed downstairs to join Jennifer, who had already taken care of the dishes, started a fresh pot of coffee, and set out small servings of dessert-seconds.

Cyndi got the large Bible Grandpa kept handy in the living room, and the three women gathered companionably around the table. The next hour in the cozy kitchen was spent opening God's Word to various verses, assuring Sally's hungry heart that God truly did love her, and that He loved Bert no matter what he'd done.

Jennifer and Cyndi explained that everyone is a sinner for whom Christ died on the cross, that each person needs to repent and accept His sacrifice and submit to Him as Savior and Lord of their life.

Before the three went upstairs to bed, Sally had surrendered herself, her life, to Jesus. With tears in her eyes she received the love that is above all loves.

The next morning at breakfast she said, "Will you please drive us home? I want to see Bert as soon as he returns . . . if he does."

While Sally and Jennifer were having second cups of coffee and Samantha was slowly spooning oatmeal, Cyndi got two empty cardboard boxes from the porch and disappeared into the large pantry. After a while she called Jennifer to help her carry them to her car.

"Is this for Sally?" Jennifer asked when they were outside.

"Yes. I wasn't sure exactly what she might need, so I put in some of most everything Grandpa had on hand."

"You must have," Jennifer said a bit breathlessly. "These boxes are really heavy."

"I know they are, but I think Sally's in real need, so besides several home-canned things, I filled empty jars with beans and cereals and pastas to help her out for a while. There's a large bowl of eggs in the refrigerator . . . don't let me forget them . . . and I want to send part of the milk Mr. Darby left a while ago."

Later, Jennifer was at the wheel, guiding her dependable

old Buick convertible to the tenant farm where Bert's family was living. Sally and Samantha were in the backseat with food boxes and milk bottles on the floor. Along the way, Cyndi described the beauty of the old mill and its surroundings.

But while she seemed to be speaking lightheartedly, an undercurrent of dread was pounding in her head, *What if Bert has come back and is mad because Sally wasn't there? What if he's drunk and has the gun? What if he thinks he has to shut me up? And what about Jennifer . . . What am I getting her into?*

Cyndi had about decided to drop Sally off on the highway where it met the lane, but realized Sally couldn't possibly get the boxes of food and milk bottles plus little Samantha to the house alone without several trips back and forth on the long, rutted drive. Cyndi prayed silently that she would know what to do if there was a confrontation with Bert, then steeled herself to be ready.

When they drove down the rutted, overgrown lane and stopped in front of the house, Cyndi noticed a man appear at the window, then duck out of sight. A few minutes later, a remorseful Bert met Sally as she climbed the steps. He took Samantha from her arms, smoothing the child's curls as he started into the house. He turned back when, instead of the car driving from the yard, the two young women got out and lugged the boxes to the porch.

"Milk's in the car." Cyndi motioned with her head, looking directly at him.

Giving Samantha to Sally, Bert sidled past Cyndi, his eyes filled with both fear and amazement as he recognized her and saw the contents of the boxes.

He probably thinks the police are right behind us to get him for battery or kidnapping, she thought.

She and Jennifer hugged Sally goodbye, waved to Samantha, and met Bert coming with the jugs of milk as they walked to the car.

"Thank ya," he said, avoiding their eyes. "Just realized

this mornin' I'd drank up all our grocery money."

Driving out the lane, Jennifer said, "After hearing him say that, I'm so glad I stuffed a twenty-dollar bill between the oatmeal and jelly jars."

"Oh, Jen, that's great! Thank you for thinking of it."

"Well, I was going to buy a new pair of shoes for the house party at Jeff's, but I'll get by with the perfectly good ones I have."

Cyndi clasped Jennifer's arm for a moment. "I'm so glad we met. You're the kind of person I've needed for a friend . . . You know, if Sally hadn't returned my tote, I'd have had to cancel my shopping entirely, but my wallet was still inside and hadn't been disturbed except for the map Sally mentioned."

That day the two young women drove to Halesburg, then shopped a little and had lunch before going to the hospital on the outskirts of town, making sure they got there as soon as visiting hours were allowed.

The visit was encouraging. Except for looking a bit wan, Tim seemed his usual cheerful self, a cast on his leg and patch on his forehead the only obvious changes.

"Bit of a leg injury and a slight concussion," he told them when they asked. "Guess I was unconscious when they found me . . . Don't know for certain how they got me out." He looked questioningly at Cyndi.

Jennifer spoke up. "The news report said they carried you up the side of a hill in a sling-stretcher, then brought you here by helicopter. I called the hospital to find out how you were doing."

"Thanks. Sort of what I thought. Sure was glad to find myself here when I came to. Dad called . . . It's too difficult for him to get in here, and I'll be home in a few days."

When that time came, Cyndi and Jennifer were at the Nichols' home to welcome him. A neighbor brought him home and they learned that the man and his wife who had been helping Tim's dad would continue with chores and meals until Tim was better able to get around.

"Sure am glad my tower's been phased out early," Tim commented, "so I don't have to be concerned about neglecting it."

Before saying goodbye, Cyndi and Jennifer finished stacking the freezer with the baked goods and casseroles they had made to help the men as they recuperated.

"I'll stop by in a week or so," Cyndi said; "but please phone if there's something I can do between visits."

"Thanks, Cyndi. I'm looking forward to a good, long talk. I'd like to be filled in on what happened after the crash. You must have gone through a lot that I'm not even aware of. Thanks to you, too, Jen. Give my regards to Lucio."

17

During a late lunch following their time of window shopping, Jennifer said, "Carlita's in bed with a virus of some sort. Thought I'd go over Monday morning and do her housework and washing. Want to come along?"

"Of course I'll come," Cyndi said. "I'll be there around nine after I've checked at the tower."

When that day arrived, they found Carlita more concerned with Juan than herself.

"I simply can't understand the change in him over the summer," she confided, worry creasing her brow. "I'm talking so quietly because Abuelita doesn't know about my fears. I don't want her to, although the other day she mentioned how withdrawn he seems lately."

"You were concerned about him a few months ago," Cyndi recalled. "Are things worse now?"

Carlita nodded. "He's always been very good in his work at school, but this term I have to urge him constantly to do his homework—even then he rarely finishes. He's been sloppy about his appearance too. Al's continually reprimanding him about it. We never had to do that before."

"Maybe it's just a normal teenage phase," Jennifer offered.

"I don't think so." Carlita's eyes revealed her worry as the two left her room.

While Jennifer mopped the kitchen and bathroom floors, Cyndi took care of the laundry. When she took Juan's clothes from the hamper in his room, her nose wrinkled at the odor emanating from them.

The two girls came again on Wednesday, cooking and baking items to put in the freezer for meals the coming week. As they worked they talked about the visit to Jeff's, now only two days away, Cyndi explaining in answer to a question of Carlita's that Mr. Darby was going to care for Grandpa's chickens while she was away.

Friday proved a fine day for traveling. Jeff and Lucio had asked Cyndi and Jennifer if they could leave at midmorning instead of in the afternoon. They agreed and the four set off amid cool breezes and sunny skies, stopping for a light lunch in Indianapolis and near Hammond for pie and coffee.

Bypassing the congestion of downtown Chicago by staying on the tollway, they passed the northern suburbs of Evanston and Wilmette, arriving in Winnetka during a glorious sunset. Following Jeff's directions, Lucio guided the car between stone pillars, up the beautiful driveway, past a perfectly manicured lawn, and parked in front of the porticoed front entrance of an impressive brick home.

Masses of petunias and ivy tumbled over the edges of large pedestaled urns stationed on either side of the walk where they got out of the car.

Although they were met at the door by a butler, Mrs. Thornburg appeared almost immediately. She welcomed each of them warmly as Jeff made the introductions.

She accompanied the two young women up a wide staircase to a hallway bordered by a balustrade, talking about activities Jeff had requested for the weekend.

"He's made reservations for all of you to have dinner out this evening, so I know you'll want to freshen up and rest a bit. I'll talk with you more in the morning," she said, smiling as she ushered them into the room they would be sharing.

"Jeff said you girls are very good friends, so I assumed you'd like a room together," she stated, a slight question in her voice.

"Thank you, Mrs. Thornburg," Cyndi returned. "That was very thoughtful. Yes, we'll enjoy being together."

"All right, then I'll leave you . . . There are double baths through those doors," she added with a gesture, pulling the door shut behind her.

Jennifer turned to Cyndi, her eyes sparkling. "Isn't this the most fabulous bedroom you've ever seen?"

Cyndi nodded, her gaze roving over the large cream and white room. Richly decorated but not overdone, it combined a sense of wealth and good taste. The patina of fine antique furniture, obviously well cared for over the years, glowed in the light from the setting sun. Blue flowers in silver bowls on the nightstands sparked the blue in the muted colors of thick oriental rugs, setting off silver and blue accessories on the dressing tables.

"It's all perfect!" Jennifer said, twirling around in the middle of the room.

"I agree! And it's really fun that we get to be together," Cyndi said, noting the satin-covered twin beds and chaises and the low, wide dressing table with a large mirror and two velvet-tufted stools. "It was so nice of Jeff to invite us."

"You know he's fallen for you, don't you?" Jennifer asked impishly.

Cyndi nodded, an uncertain look in her eyes as she turned to answer a knock on the door.

Jeff stood there, a pleasant grin on his face. "Thought you'd like to have these right away," he said, as he stepped in and put their suitcases on luggage stands at the foot of each bed. Then striding back to the door, he added, "Lucio and I will meet you in the small study in an hour. Does that give you enough time?"

They nodded and he informed them on his way out, "It's

the second door to the left off the foyer at the bottom of the stairs."

True to their word, a little less than an hour later the two girls were descending the staircase, both feeling elegant and sophisticated in their evening gowns and sparkling jewelry.

When they paused in the study doorway, Jeff's and Lucio's eyes told them they were as pretty as they hoped.

Jeff drove them to dinner in a long, low-slung silver-gray Mercedes. The motor purred quietly as they swept out of the drive and along the highway in superb comfort.

The evening began with dinner in the small, beautifully appointed dining room of a large, old hotel—a landmark soon to make way for a more modern building, Jeff told them.

"I hate to see it torn down," he stated after their orders had been taken. "It has nice memories for me. My folks used to bring me here when I was young."

"I can understand your nostalgia," Cyndi affirmed. "I feel a little like that about the old fire tower, even though it can hardly compare to this place. The tower has served its purpose well, but it is being replaced by something that can do the job even better. It was part of my childhood dreams and, this year, my work, but Tim Nichols said the helicopter not only saves man-hours but is extremely efficient for spotting fires. The chopper can also be used in some fire-fighting situations."

"They're proving to be effective tools in areas of our work, too," Lucio added.

Jennifer questioned with a light laugh, "You chase speeders with a helicopter? Doesn't seem quite fair."

Lucio grinned at her. "There are times, Jen, when that wouldn't be a bad idea. But seriously, we're learning to use them in critical areas of our work. Things can be seen from the air that would be missed at ground level."

"That's certainly true," Cyndi agreed. "Tim took me up

one day, and I had an entirely different perspective of the area . . . enjoyed it, too."

"Oh, that sounds interesting!" Jennifer exclaimed. "I'd like to go up sometime. Do you think he'd take me? Would you ask him, Lucio?"

"I'll check with him. I've been wishing for an overview myself." Then with a quick, inquisitive glance, he added, "Might be interesting, huh, Jeff?"

Jeff nodded thoughtfully, then grinned at Jennifer's almost childlike anticipation.

They changed the subject and began chatting about Lucio and Jennifer's coming wedding in which Cyndi was to be the maid of honor and Jeff the best man.

Following their leisurely dinner, the young couples attended a concert by a visiting symphony orchestra, then took a drive along the shore of Lake Michigan, stopping for a while to watch the display of colored lights shining from beneath Buckingham Fountain. "Looks a bit like liquid Jell-O," Lucio quipped. "But beautiful, really beautiful."

Cyndi was thoroughly enjoying the evening's events and the time with her friends. She was intensely aware of a special gentleness in Jeff's attitude toward her, a deep something in his eyes when she met his gaze. She wasn't sure if that pleased or disturbed her. She was certain he was soon going to speak to her about his feelings, but she was also quite sure she wasn't ready to hear what he was going to say. She didn't even know how she would respond.

Help me do and say the right thing, Lord, she prayed silently as they settled themselves in the car for the pleasant drive under the stars back to Jeff's home.

Although it was late when they arrived, they strolled along the walks of the small but lovely estate in the bright moonlight.

Lucio walked with his arm around Jennifer's shoulders. A few paces behind them Jeff pulled Cyndi's arm under his, leaving his hand on hers where it rested on his arm.

"Cyndi," he said quietly, "there's something I want to talk to you about. I'm sure you know what it is . . . Is now the right time?"

She didn't raise her head to look at him but answered softly, "Jeff, I'd rather you didn't just now."

She barely heard his soft sigh as he stopped walking for a moment. Then gently squeezing her hand, he said, "It's all right, I'll wait."

"Thank you, Jeff," Cyndi whispered.

Returning to the house they found the welcoming glow of shaded lamps in the study, and decided to relax awhile before retiring. A small fire burned in the fireplace in front of which were grouped comfortable upholstered armchairs. Sinking into one of them, Cyndi commented, "What a relaxing room." Surrounding her were shelves of books, a desk with a high-backed chair, a sideboard with its polished surface holding pitchers of iced juices and a silver tray of cookies and sliced fruitcake. The low coffee table before her stood ready with fine china plates and crystal goblets.

"Looks as though Mom expected us to be hungry," Jeff said as he began serving his guests.

Cyndi pictured him as a little boy growing up in this house, taking the affluence for granted. She wondered if it was a Christian home. Maybe his parents were just enjoying their resources and life in this world without a thought about God and eternal life. She found out the following morning.

Breakfast was served in the dining room to accommodate the family and their guests. Jeff's younger brother, Sam, and sister, Janie, were both home for the weekend and each had brought a friend from college.

They met Jeff's father, a congenial, distinguished-looking man whose dark hair was graying at the temples. He lowered himself into the chair at the head of the long, oval table opposite his wife.

After everyone was seated, while commenting on the delectable aromas from the kitchen, Mr. Thornburg opened a small Bible saying, "As has been the custom in our home since we were married, we'd like to share a psalm from God's Word before breakfast. This one, the twenty-ninth, is a hymn of praise to the Lord:

> Praise the Lord you angels of his;
> Praise his glory and his strength.
> Praise him for his majestic glory,
> the glory of his name.
> Come before him clothed in sacred garments.

All was quiet around the table as the resonant voice continued through the verses to the last paragraph. Mr. Thornburg paused then and said, "This great, almighty God cared about me enough to send His Son to die for my sins. And He cares that much for each of you. Listen to this:

> At the flood, the Lord showed his control of all creation. Now he continues to unveil his power. He will give his people strength. He will bless them with peace.

He closed the Bible and smiled at his wife. She looked searchingly at those gathered around the table before saying, "I have a dear friend who is very worried about a problem her son has. I would like us to pray about this.

"Do any of you have a problem, some difficulty you want us to mention as we pray?" She looked questioningly at the young people.

Cyndi's thoughts went immediately to Carlita and her worry over Juan, but because Lucio was there, she said nothing; he might not be aware of his sister's concern, of Juan's problem—if there was a problem.

Sam asked to be remembered concerning a decision he needed to make about a course at college.

When no one else added a request, Mr. Thornburg spoke briefly to the Lord about the things mentioned and asked His blessing on the food they were about to eat.

When he raised his head, he looked at Mrs. Thornburg, who quietly left the table and returned a few moments later with a spritely middle-aged lady, both of them bearing large platters that they placed on each end of the table.

"Cyndi, I believe you and Jennifer are the only ones who haven't met Mrs. Zehner. She's been part of my life since I was a tiny girl. It was she who taught me to cook and even led me to the Lord Jesus."

Smiles and nods acknowledged the introduction before Mrs. Zehner returned to the kitchen. They all enjoyed the bountiful breakfast she'd prepared for them, filling their plates with fluffy scrambled eggs, sausages and crisp bacon, puffy mushroom omelets, tiny buckwheat pancakes, and blueberry muffins.

The buffet held a chafing dish of hot cereal, pitchers of cold milk and juices, and a large urn of coffee.

The congenial group was obviously enjoying each other's company as well as the delicious breakfast so they lingered long around the table. Cyndi was completely relaxed and comfortable, knowing without a single doubt that she could enjoy belonging to this family that loved the Lord. Yes, she could actually picture herself as Jeff's wife.

It would be so easy to let him speak about it, she thought, *And I don't feel that it would be wrong . . . I care deeply for Jeff. So why am I so hesitant?*

Jeff leaned over to ask quietly, "Why so pensive? You look as if you have the weight of the world on your shoulders."

"Sorry," Cyndi said. "Guess my mind was wandering for a minute. But it *was* the weight of the world on my mind—my world anyway."

Seeing the concerned questioning in his eyes, she smiled quickly. "It's nothing that won't be resolved eventually and the Lord will guide me in that, I'm sure." Then, in a more lighthearted tone, she added, "Your mother said we're all going to the Chicago Art Institute this morning. I'm looking forward to it."

Shortly after noon the group emerged from their tour of the Institute into the sunlight, descending the wide steps between two lifelike statues of lions guarding its entrance.

"It's unusual and very nice the way your parents seem to enjoy their children's friends," Cyndi remarked to Jeff.

"It's always been that way," he answered. "From the time we were very young, we were included in some of their social events, and they were always available as party planners as well as being good listeners to us and our friends. I still enjoy their company and respect them immensely."

"David and I were fortunate to have fairly open relationships with our folks, too," Cyndi said. "Plus we had our grandmother, who was always ready to listen to our troubles and dreams when we were with her."

On the drive back to the Thornburg home, Mr. Thornburg took the passenger seat next to Jeff, who drove the luxurious van that furnished comfortable seating for the whole group. Jeff's mother sat beside Cyndi, and during the drive learned about Cyndi and her family.

A simple lunch was served beneath large umbrellas at stone tables on the lawn. Dessert was a medley of fresh fruits and chocolate meringue cups filled with minted whipped cream, which Cyndi especially enjoyed.

They all talked for a while after the meal before going to their rooms for a rest before tennis and lawn games.

Early evening found the group dressed for dinner out, followed by a musical. The elder Thornburgs had settled into the study adjoining their bedroom upstairs to prepare for their Sunday school classes the next day.

Their church, Cyndi discovered the following morning, was an imposing limestone structure with ornate stained glass windows, built late in the last century.

Majestic strains from a large pipe organ filled the vaulted space.

"Have you always attended church here?" Cyndi whispered to Jeff as he escorted her to the pew in which his parents had just seated themselves.

"Yes," he answered softly. "As a baby I was dedicated to the Lord here. When I was twelve, I gave my life to Him voluntarily at that altar."

As the service progressed, Cyndi realized that although the surroundings were vastly different from the small churches she was used to, the hymns were familiar and the sermon from God's Word penetrated the hearts of the listeners.

Standing beside Jeff, singing the closing song from the hymnbook he held, her thoughts slipped to the many times during the past two days his eyes seemed to show how he felt about her. She realized how simple and right it would seem to just say yes to him and quit brooding over the matter.

Sunday dinner was quite formal. It was served midafternoon in the dining room with additional guests. The Thornburgs' pastor and wife had been invited, as well as a neighbor couple to whom they'd been witnessing about the Lord.

It evidently isn't a matter of either-or, Cyndi thought as she finished her dessert. *It's not absolutely necessary to give up a life of financial security in order to live for God, to express His love. Maybe He's placed some people in wealthier positions so they'll be there to witness to other rich people.*

I guess it was mainly my eagerness for financial gain, making it the goal of my life, that was wrong . . . It had even pushed fellowship with God out of my routine.

Just before they left, Mrs. Thornburg hugged Cynthia warmly. "If you haven't definite plans to be with relatives for Thanksgiving, will you consider spending the weekend here with us? I know Jeff, as well as the rest of the family, would very much like you to."

Surprised at the unexpected invitation, Cyndi stepped back, hesitating a moment, her thoughts in a jumble.

"May I please let you know later, Mrs. Thornburg?"

"Certainly, my dear, but we hope your answer will be yes," she replied.

18

The first thing Cyndi did Monday morning after breakfast and caring for Grandpa's chickens was to write a thank-you note to Jeff's mother, enclosing a sketch done from memory of the elder Thornburgs beside the picturesque gazebo on their back lawn. Then she phoned the Nichols' home to see how Tim and his dad were doing.

Tim answered, exuberantly happy to hear from her.

"Been trying to reach you over the weekend—sure glad you're all right." Then in answer to her question, he said, "I'm getting along great. Leg's healing much quicker than expected and the old head seems okay, too."

He suggested a time for her to be at his home that evening so she could fill him in on what happened after the crash. Before saying goodbye he asked, "Have you decided definitely about not returning to college this semester?"

"I'm not going. I've told Grandpa I'll keep an eye on things here and stay at the tower for a while yet. And since I'm to be here, I'll be in Jennifer and Lucio's wedding."

Cyndi arrived at the Nichols' home loaded down with food. She came earlier than they expected, ready to surprise them by preparing dinner.

As the evening progressed, Cyndi realized once again how contented she felt in this small home with these two friends. Even though it was simple compared with Jeff's family mansion, she experienced the same underlying sense of love and sharing in both homes.

It must be because the families in both places are living by God's Spirit, she decided.

Later, when Tim walked with her to her car, leaning heavily on a cane, he spoke with deep feeling in his voice, "I've missed you, Cyndi, very much." Then, in a lighter tone, "Doc said I can get rid of this cane in another day or so. How about a picnic at the mill later this week? It will probably be the last one this season with so many things going on and the weather turning cold."

"Okay, let's do that, Tim. I'll prepare all the food this time. Call me later and we'll decide on the day."

When they arrived at the stream's edge opposite the mill and spread the blanket on the woody grass, Cyndi noted the changes in the weeks since they'd been there. Only the long, strappy leaves and slim, dried stalks remained from the earlier masses of orange day lilies, but their color was replaced by the yellow, orange, and red of the fall leaves. Tall, stately cattails decorated the edge of the stream.

Cyndi and Tim, warm in jeans and heavy pullover sweaters, munched on meatloaf sandwiches, baked beans, and boiled eggs. They sipped hot chocolate and saw in each other's eyes the joy of being together.

Yet as Cyndi glanced up a bit later after uncovering a plate of apple tarts, she saw the shadow of something else fill his eyes. Then pulling his gaze away and taking a tart, Tim said, almost too casually, "Lucio Gembe went with me on a fly-over in the copter yesterday. We squeezed his girlfriend Jennifer in, too."

"I'm glad they got the chance," Cyndi said. "They mentioned that they'd really like the opportunity."

Then in a sort of forced, off-hand manner, Tim added,

"They said you all had been guests at that Jeff guy's home."

"Jeff Thornburg," Cyndi supplied. "We had a really great time. His family has a beautiful home. Jen and I shared a gorgeous room."

"Different from what you're used to, but the lifestyle you've always dreamed of, huh?" Tim asked, his eyes focused on the stream.

"Very different," Cyndi agreed. "They're fairly wealthy, I guess. Everything was the best in a refined sort of way."

Tim kept his eyes averted, listening.

"Jeff's parents seem to be fine Christian people . . . his brother and sister, too," Cyndi continued. "We all had a lot of fun together and some serious discussions."

When Tim said nothing, she changed the subject. "Where did you take Lucio and Jen on the flight?"

"I was to do a time-trial test run over the entire forest, so I took them along, but Lucio seemed especially interested in the area north of your tower. I hadn't realized he was interested in forest management. He asked me to do two extra passes over each of the areas where we had the nighttime fires last spring . . . remember?"

Remember? Cyndi reflected silently. *How could I forget when those areas and my tower had been marked on a map, the very areas where the fires occurred?*

"Yes, I do," she said aloud. "I wonder what interested him so? Did he say?"

"No, he didn't. There was lush growth in both places now, unusual because it seemed to be all one type of plant. There's normally a mixture of growing flora."

"Well, he did grow up around here just like you," she reasoned. "I suppose it was intriguing seeing it from the air."

"True," Tim said. "But those were the only spots where he asked for extra-low altitude passes."

"Perhaps those areas had some special meaning to him as a child, the way the mill area has for you."

"Could be," Tim agreed as Cyndi began gathering together the dishes, putting them into the picnic hamper and folding the tablecloth.

When she looked up, he was looking searchingly at her.

"Cyndi, does he mean a lot to you?" he asked, his earnestness evident in his voice.

"He?" she questioned.

"Jeff . . . Are you in love with him?"

19

Startled at the suddenness of the question, Cyndi stared at him, not knowing how to respond.

Do I love Jeff? Do I care about him the way Tim means?

She dropped her gaze to her lap. *What can I say?* she wondered, her thoughts skittering over all the aspects of the relationship she had been questioning for days.

Cyndi looked up then, her brown eyes gazing frankly, steadily into his blue ones. "I don't know, Ace," she admitted very softly. "I honestly don't know."

Tim breathed a deep sigh, was silent a few moments, then a small smile touched his lips as he reached out to take her hand.

"Okay," he said quietly, "I had to ask . . . Forgive me if I was prying."

Cyndi's intense countenance softened with an answering smile; her hand pressed the fingers entwined with hers. "No, you weren't prying; it's all right that you asked."

Tim stood, his hand still clasping hers, and pulled her up, "Let's put these things on the stump over there till we get back. I want to show you something by the mill."

They crossed the bridge spanning the stream and as they approached the stone structure, Cyndi noticed that the undergrowth had been removed from around it, the door was no longer sagging on its hinges, and a lower window had its glass replaced.

"Oh, Tim!" she exclaimed. "You wanted so much to get

this property someday. Has someone bought it before you had a chance?"

"No, but I'm starting to make my move, trying to interest some people in backing the Nature Center idea with financial help. It looks promising."

"I'm so glad!" Cyndi exclaimed as she turned to give him a quick hug. "It's really great."

"That hug wasn't so bad either." He grinned as she dropped her arms and turned to touch the cool gray stone wall, almost covered with the red tones of the Virginia-creeper vine displaying its autumn colors.

"Thanks for caring, Cyndi."

"Well, it's such a good idea, Tim. If your moth and artifact collections are any indication of the interest you'll pass on to others, this will be a valuable area to the community . . . probably the entire state eventually."

"Hold on, Cyndi," he laughed. "Those are grand thoughts, but I haven't even started yet, may not get to. But if I do, it'll be a lot of work and it will take a long time to get established."

"You can do it, Tim," she encouraged, turning toward him. "I know you can. I have faith in your ability."

"Do you?" he said softly, putting his hands on her shoulders, looking deep into her eyes. "You really do believe I can? I needed that assurance. It means more to me than you know."

He bent to kiss her gently on the forehead, then took her by the hand to walk around the mill where he pointed out some spots, sharing with her his ideas for reconstruction of the historic mill and development of its surroundings.

Although Cyndi was paying attention to what he was saying, her mind was also considering another point—the question he'd asked about Jeff, her feelings about him. She knew she had to resolve it soon. Even more pressing after being with him again was how she felt about Tim. She decided she had to take a specific time away from both of them to examine her heart, to pray and ask God's definite guidance as she came to a decision.

"Cyndi?" Tim broke her concentration.

"What?"

"I asked what you thought about a viewing window in the nature museum facing the area where the stream is separated from the forest by that expanse of year-round wildflowers. Folks could relax in comfortable chairs and view the wildlife that passes here, probably using one-way glass so the animals wouldn't be startled."

"Sounds nice," Cyndi said, trying to bring her attention back to the present topic.

Returning to the van they heard the lovely whistled melody of a red-winged blackbird as it made its undulating flight overhead to land in a maple tree ahead of them. Just then a shaft of light from the setting sun touched the yellow leaves.

"Look like tiny flames of fire, don't they?" Cyndi commented.

"Yes, but thankfully they're not treacherous," Tim said. "We'll have to be keeping a closer watch now for fires. It's sometimes bad in an autumn following such a dry summer."

"Now that you'll be using the helicopter, will I be needed in the tower much longer?" she asked.

"Sure will. We're just starting to utilize the new method. My tower's the only one closed until we've figured a sure schedule for good coverage. Experienced people in the tower are valuable. We don't want to become overconfident with the copter and maybe overlook some crucial aspect of reconnaissance."

Then as an afterthought he asked, "Were you anxious to relinquish your tower duty, Cyndi?" Other questions in his eyes lay behind the spoken one.

"No, not really," she answered slowly. "In one way, I hate to see it end."

"And the other way?" he prompted.

She spoke the words as though they were being forced from her. "I just wondered . . . if I wanted to leave . . . what my obligation here would be."

"I see," Tim replied quietly, reserve creeping into his voice. "You'd be under no obligation, Cyndi. We'd work something out here to take over for you."

She had a nagging feeling that she'd upset him, somehow thrown a wet blanket on their day, yet she had no idea what to say to make things better. With a pang she realized she might hurt him badly with her decision concerning Jeff.

Cyndi didn't sleep much that night and when she did, her dreams were troubled. The next morning she lifted her heart in prayer, asking God to enable her to sort out her emotions and come to a definite decision about Jeff—*before* she'd have to respond to his mother's invitation for Thanksgiving.

The next day she had just finished her calculations at the tower when the phone rang.

"Redbud, this is Bill over in Bluebird tower. Just wanted to say hi. Since Tim's tower is closed, you and I will be in touch occasionally. This is what I call a golden morning with the leaves glittering in the sunshine. It doesn't happen often and it won't last long, either."

That night it rained and by the time Cyndi had to man the tower again, most of the leaves were on the ground. She had climbed the long flights of stairs and was gazing through the windows checking the countryside.

Summer is certainly over, autumn has arrived, and Jennifer's wedding is coming up, she realized.

An unusually warm, drying wind blew the next few days; many weed-flower heads became crisp, popping their seedcases to expose bountiful food for the birds and field mice. Black walnuts, hazelnuts, butternuts, and pine cones plopped to the ground.

Mr. Darby left a pumpkin on the back steps with the milk, giving Cyndi the idea of baking pies, taking one to Tim and his dad and some to Carlita's family. After a quick check of the cupboard and pantry confirmed a shortage of the needed spices, she decided to drive to the store that evening after leaving the tower.

Entering the outskirts of Milltown, she turned the car onto the street where the Hernandez family lived, thinking to tell Carlita she would be dropping off some pies the following afternoon. As she drove up to their home she noticed a police car in the drive. Although it wasn't the one she'd seen the times Lucio had been there, she decided not to stop. She was hesitant about possibly meeting Jeff right now when she was so unsure of their relationship. She could phone Carlita instead.

Continuing on to the store, she quickly made her few purchases, picking up the afternoon issue of the local newspaper at the checkout.

Later, while the pies were cooling, she settled down at the kitchen table to read the paper while eating a late supper. The rising wind blowing leaves and twigs against the windows made her feel cozy and protected in the homey kitchen.

A front-page article about problems of the school board was overshadowed by one below the heading *Marijuana Pickers Arrested.*

Cyndi began reading it with interest because of Jeff and Lucio's conversations on the subject with her and Jennifer.

> An Indiana State Trooper with local officers has arrested several out-of-state marijuana pickers in two areas of the forest north of Milltown.
>
> Although the State Police Drug Patrol had destroyed much of the illegal ditch weed in our area before harvest, the plots confiscated in these arrests were obviously planted and cultivated.
>
> Of the people arrested, two are local juveniles whose

> names will not be made public. They have been remanded to the custody of their parents until their appearances in juvenile court.

Cyndi's gaze ran quickly over the paragraph listing unfamiliar names of the adults arrested before she turned to page two where the account was continued.

> The juveniles were evidently not acquainted with the adult pickers discovered in the first large patch, but had been taken to the second area by a local man for whom they had been working during the summer, a man they knew only as "twenty-seven."

20

"Twenty-seven!" Cynthia gasped, wondering if there was some connection between the two nighttime fires and the marijuana growing in the plots. She wondered also what would happen to the two young people and whether they knew what they were doing. Then she continued reading.

> A pair of State Troopers, working in the area earlier but not here at the time of the arrests, have felt someone in this general area might be connected with a large mid-western narcotics ring. The use of an alias by at least one person seems to point in that direction.
>
> There is conjecture also regarding the probable use of a light plane in removing the contraband material from this area.

Although Cyndi immediately chided herself for the unbidden thought, Tim and the delivery with the little plane the day of the crash immediately leaped into her mind.

"But he couldn't be involved in anything illegal," she assured herself. "I just know he wouldn't even consider it."

To reassure herself further, she went into the living room and dialed Tim's phone number, waiting impatiently while it rang and rang. Eventually she heard the receiver lifted and his dad answered her inquiry.

"No, he isn't here, Cyndi . . . Won't be for at least several days. Guess he's quite involved with the mill plans. Said you and the Bluebird tower could pretty well cover his former area for a while."

"I see," she said slowly, not seeing at all as she forced a pleasant goodbye before hanging up.

Of course it's something to do with his hopes for the mill, she thought. *What else would take him away from his responsibilities? I should be ashamed for even letting the idea enter my mind.*

But many times that night and the next day she had to push the ugly, frightening insinuation of his possible involvement from her mind.

The questions were forced from her thoughts suddenly when the phone in the tower rang just as she was about to leave that evening.

"Redbud, Bill at Bluebird. We've got what looks like a real breakout with a fire they've been fighting over the ridge from here. We'll need all the help we can get before the night's over, I'm afraid. Fire department from Milltown's being notified. Ours is already on location. Could you try to contact Tim Nichols? I couldn't reach him . . . and be ready yourself."

"Okay," Cyndi replied, excitement stirring. "Tim's away, but I can leave right now. Where should I meet you?"

"I need to stay here awhile yet to direct the incoming fighters. Meet me here at the tower. Follow Route Seven and turn left onto the gravel road just after you pass Rangeline. Bring some drinking water if you have any handy containers."

"All right. Be there soon as I can," she agreed after receiving additional instructions.

At her grandfather's house, Cyndi hurriedly changed into old jeans, heavy boots, and a thick, hooded sweatshirt with a bandana around her neck.

She quickly slipped the pies into a hamper and after filling several clean, empty milk jugs with water and ice cubes, she lugged them to the car. She also threw in a wire rake and a pair of old gloves from the back porch. Speeding away in the twilight, she gladly remembered that she'd filled the car's gas tank while in town.

That faint, thin line on the horizon I kept checking all day must have been haze from the fire, she said to herself as she crossed Route Four and angled off on 258 south. A moment later as the sound of a siren approached from behind, she pulled over on the shoulder just as a pair of firetrucks thundered by—lights flashing, sirens shrieking.

Unfamiliar with the area, Cyndi drove more carefully now, closely watching crossroad signs and checking them with a flashlight as dusk closed in. Then she verified her way by the rough map sketch she'd made while Bill was giving directions.

On Route Seven now, the smell of smoke was beginning to reach her, although she couldn't see it yet.

Cyndi estimated she'd driven another twenty miles or so when she began to see the glow in the sky. The odor of smoke, more pungent than ever, soon began seeping into the car.

Passing the marker for Rangeline Road, she found the left turnoff Bill had described. The wheels crunched on the gravel as she maneuvered around the curves in the early darkness between stands of tall pines.

When she pulled into the parking lot, her headlights made a sweep over the clearing and the tower's spindly looking legs. Pulling onto the parking strip, she saw a downward shaft of light from the trapdoor as Bill exited at the top of the stairs.

"Okay if we go in your car?" he shouted, sprinting over after reaching the bottom.

"Sure!" Cyndi opened her door, then scooted over to the passenger side. "You drive. You know the way."

"Glad to see you're dressed for the job," Bill commented, car wheels spinning on the gravel as he accelerated down the road.

"Hope you have your hard hat handy," he added.

"It's in the backseat. I always keep it there," Cyndi replied. "What about the fire? What's happening?"

"They're not sure how it started. Think it may have been

from a negligent camper or smoker. Had it contained this afternoon, but thick smoke kept them from seeing right away that it had jumped the backfired area near the little village of Rabbitrun. They're doing more backfiring now and trying to plow and bulldoze extra sections surrounding it, hoping to save the homes."

"Do you think they can?" Cyndi asked anxiously as she watched the wide red expanse in the sky overlaid with a black cloud even darker than the night around them.

"Don't know . . . They closed the schools this morning," Bill answered, slowing, then stopping to make way for a line of cars emerging from a side road.

"Folks leaving Rabbitrun, evidently," he concluded.

Cyndi rolled the window down for a better view. Acrid smoke poured in and she quickly rolled it back up.

Bill pulled onto the side road, soon made a sharp turn out of the tree area they were in and Cyndi gasped.

"Looks like the entire countryside's on fire!"

"Sure gives that impression, doesn't it? But I've seen worse," Bill said, slowing the car to drive cautiously around several families walking along the shoulder of the road. Everyone, even the children, carried bundles of their possessions.

Bill moved the car slowly ahead, passing houses silhouetted against the eerie redness. A sheriff's car, public address system blaring, was driving through the area urging residents to evacuate.

"Heard they've set up a temporary shelter at the community auction barn, which is well on the outskirts of town, away from the fire danger," Bill commented.

At the far end of the street he pulled over to where several trucks were parked and a large group of men were milling around.

Cyndi's eyes began to adjust to the strange red-gray atmosphere. In the brightness from headlights, she saw weary-faced men in hard hats wearing kerchiefs around their necks with an extra one hanging from the back of the hats to protect their necks.

She climbed out of the car and retrieved her hat from the backseat while Bill stepped over to speak to one of the men. Returning moments later, he said, "They're shuttling groups around to give a bit of relief to the hardest working ones; we're to go out with the crew leaving now in that truck."

Gathering up her rake and gloves and jamming the hard hat on her head, Cyndi said, "Tell them there's pie and ice water in my car."

"You're okay, Cyndi," Bill grinned, turning to relay her message before they clambered up into the back of the truck already filling with firefighters.

The next hours were wearing, at times frightening, for Cyndi. Eyes stinging, faces streaked with soot, the group worked together, beaters flaying, fires hissing as spray hit them from nozzles of backpack pumps strapped to some of the fighters' backs.

Using her rake, Cyndi followed a line of men, making sure the ashes from the flames they'd soaked and then beaten were completely dead.

Late the next morning, following a warm, soapy bath to remove the soot and ease her fatigued body, her eyes red-rimmed and dark-circled, Cyndi crawled into bed too tired to eat, wanting only to sleep.

A few days later Mr. Darby left the current copy of the newspaper with the milk and a penciled note:

> Heard you helped in this fire; might like to read about it.

Because rain had fallen steadily the previous night, Cyndi was relieved of tower duty, so she settled down for a leisurely breakfast. After doing the dishes and pouring another cup of coffee, she unfolded the paper. Pictures of the fire and Rabbitrun's evacuation brought that night's events vividly to her memory. She hoped she'd never have to go through that again.

Glad to read there had been no serious injuries, her glance continued down the column.

> A handful of firefighters kept watch against any breakouts until the rains started. Cause of the fire is still under investigation. Damages to the state game preserve and private woodlands have not yet been estimated.

Then Cyndi saw the heading of a double-column story halfway down the page proclaiming another arrest in the marijuana investigation. Staring at her from the paper was a photo of Bert—the man who had several times caused her fear and uncertainty . . . Bert, the vicious loudmouth . . . Bert, the sometimes gentle person.

I should visit Sally, Cyndi immediately decided. *Maybe there's something I can do to help her.*

Hurriedly packing a box with eggs, a loaf of bread, the pies she'd baked the previous evening, and a jar of milk, she carried it to her car. Driving to Sally's she realized she hadn't taken time to read the story accompanying Bert's picture.

Sally opened the door warily, but swung it open in a glad welcome when she saw Cyndi standing there. Tears filled her eyes and ran down her cheeks when Cyndi put her arm around her shoulders, saying, "I'm sorry about Bert."

They sat together on the couch. Slowly Sally told about her husband's arrest.

"He was stopped by a police officer on the edge of town the other evening 'cause the old truck's taillight was broke—warned him to get it fixed.

"Seems the officer smelled something strange in the truck cab and noticed a bunch of plastic garbage bags on the truck bed. He didn't mention it then but followed my Bert at a distance."

Sally paused, shaking her head sadly. "He was messed up in illegal things worse'n I guessed. Arrested him delivering marijuana to a little airstrip somewhere around here.

"The officer kindly drove out here to tell me or I wouldn't have known what happened. Said Bert at first wasn't going to tell where he was living, but guess he realized me and little Samantha out here alone would need to know. I'll maybe have to leave here if he's sent away." Sally's shoulders drooped.

"Where would you go?" Cyndi asked.

"Don't know . . . back to my folks in Illinois, I suppose. But I'll be so 'shamed."

"It's not your fault, Sally," Cyndi comforted. "Would you like to come home with me for a few days?"

"That'd be nice," Sally answered slowly, almost accepting, "but I keep hoping maybe Potter isn't as sly and mean as Bert said . . . Thought he might stop by with some money. He's not paid Bert anything lately that I know of."

"But, Sally, if Bert's been arrested, surely Mr. Potter will be too."

"Don't know. The officer said Bert wouldn't reveal the name of his boss, so I didn't say anything either. I don't want Bert mad at me whenever he gets back."

"I'll remember to pray for you, Sally, asking God to show you what to do. I honestly think it would be better for Bert if Potter were exposed.

"I'm to be in a friend's wedding on Friday," she continued, "but I'll come by Sunday morning to get you and Samantha for church and dinner."

Thursday evening at the wedding rehearsal Cyndi noticed that Juan seemed overly quiet and withdrawn, carrying out in silence instructions for ushering the next evening, not even entering into the joyous bantering later at the Hernandez home.

Cyndi observed, too, the drawn look on Carlita's face, the deep worry in her eyes that she couldn't completely hide from her friend's scrutiny.

After the others were busy with conversation and refreshments, Cyndi drew her aside.

"What's wrong, Carlita?" she asked gently. "Let me share whatever's troubling you."

Carlita nodded to her to follow, leading the way to her sewing-laundry room and shutting the door behind them.

"You will know soon, anyway," she said, turning to face Cyndi. "Everyone will . . . word gets around. I need to know a Christian friend is praying for me, for us."

"Go on," Cyndi encouraged when Carlita hesitated.

After clearing her throat, Carlita asked, "You've heard about the marijuana arrests?"

"I read about them in the paper," Cyndi answered.

"My Juan was one of them, one of the juveniles mentioned."

Cyndi said nothing, but put her arm around her friend.

Carlita continued. "Al was working late when the police came and he doesn't know. I promised Juan I would say nothing to the family until after the wedding. Ever since he was a tiny boy, Lucio has been his hero; they were always very close until Lucio moved away for his work with the State Police.

"Juan's full of remorse and says he's disgracing the family and might cause problems for his Uncle Lucio. He's sure he'll shame Lucio in the eyes of his co-workers."

Tears filled Carlita's eyes. "My poor Juan . . . He was always such a good boy."

Cyndi drew Carlita close, patting her shoulder, searching for words she couldn't find to offer reassurance and comfort.

Oh, God, she prayed silently, *give Carlita strength to bear whatever she has to face.*

Wiping her eyes, Carlita said, "Juan and Dan are to appear before the juvenile authorities next Friday, the day after

Lucio and Jennifer return from their short honeymoon trip. I'm glad for their sakes the hearing was delayed so it won't spoil their happy time."

"I'll come and stay with Luz and your grandmother that afternoon," Cyndi offered. "I know it'll be a difficult day for you."

The wedding the next evening was beautiful. Cyndi's dress was a gorgeous teal green taffeta, and as the maid of honor, she followed the trail of flower petals little Luz had sprinkled down the aisle.

Jennifer followed, looking enchanting in her white satin bridal gown. The look of love in Lucio's eyes when he gazed at Jennifer made Cyndi's heart pound.

Will anyone ever look at me that way? she thought and glanced over at Jeff. *He looks so handsome in his black tuxedo.* The pastor's voice broke into her thoughts, and she turned to face the altar as the ceremony began.

A week later, Jennifer phoned Friday morning to say they'd returned, happily chattering about the trip and expressing a wish to visit together soon.

They evidently don't know about Juan yet, Cyndi thought, replacing the receiver.

Because of the softly falling rain, she hadn't gone to the tower and would be able to devote the afternoon to the Hernandez home as promised. Juan and his parents were to be in the judge's chambers at one-thirty, so Cyndi planned to be at their place by one o'clock.

Happy to see Jennifer's car parked in front, she pulled in behind it. As she started up the walk, she saw the emergency vehicle in the driveway and an unfamiliar car beside it.

Grandmother Evetia must be ill, Cyndi feared, hurrying up the front steps, knocking quickly.

Jennifer opened the door, her eyes wide with horror, her

mouth working crazily as she tried to speak.

"What is it, Jen? What's happened?" Cyndi asked, grasping Jennifer's shoulders.

Jennifer gasped back a sob. "Juan . . . it's Juan. He wasn't at the table for lunch . . . Lucio just found him." She choked back her tears. Then when she could speak she added tonelessly, "He's dead, Cyndi . . . He took his own life."

21

The following days were filled with drizzling rain, many questions, and heavy heartache. Cyndi took little Luz home with her until after the funeral Sunday afternoon, knowing that Jennifer and Lucio were at the Hernandez home to receive mourning neighbors and friends, to accept donations of food, and serve meals that were barely touched.

Cyndi wished Tim were home. She longed to see him, to put her head on his shoulder and let herself cry. When the vague suspicion of his possible drug involvement tried to intrude on her thoughts, she pushed it aside.

Carlita didn't want Luz at the funeral, not knowing yet how to explain Juan's death to her. Evetia stayed home, too, wanting only to remember her Juan as the fine, loving, laughing boy she had known since his birth . . . the boy who would now live only in her memories. Cyndi sat quietly on the stool near Evetia's rocking chair while Luz slept.

Evetia sat dry-eyed, her shawl fastened at her throat with a small flower pin Juan had given her for her birthday, her hands folded in her lap. The rocker moved slowly back and forth. When she finally spoke, her voice was frail and whispery.

"Never will I understand why this happened, how it could happen. There are no more tears in me to cry. Yet, some way, somehow, even in this thing beyond our imagination, our God can eventually bring something good from some aspect of it."

She was silent awhile, rocking gently. Cyndi reached out to touch her hand.

"How do I know this?" Evetia questioned quietly: "I know because I've lived many years, have seen many tragedies . . . though none that cut so deeply. Always God gives His children strength and courage to carry on if they look to Him.

"Then one day someone's heart is touched by Him because of the hurt and trial through which they've passed and they are able to see their need of Him in their lives also."

Evetia's dark eyes turned to look into Cyndi's. "You are so young. You must try to understand that God doesn't cause our tragedies, but sometimes uses them eventually in His wisdom to bring the blessing of His presence to others."

Evetia's glance dropped to her hands. "Juan was the light of my life. I had such plans for him." Her shoulders shook with hard, dry sobs. Tears streaming down her cheeks, Cynthia knelt, gathering Cyndi into her arms; together they mourned.

Jennifer phoned several days later to tell Cyndi about Al's leave of absence from his job and that he was taking the family to Mexico for a while.

"They've been saving for a long time as a surprise for Grandmother Evetia, so she could visit Cheran and see her beloved Tarascan Mountains again," she explained. "Now—now they just need to get away from the place of hurt for a while."

She paused and Cyndi could tell her friend was trying to compose herself.

"Carlita said to give you her love, her heartfelt thanks for standing by her, and to tell you goodbye."

After Jennifer and Lucio had returned to his post in the northern part of the state and Tim was still away, Cyndi was at loose ends. She felt lonely and took little interest in her work at the tower or even in her sketching.

After a visit with Sally revealed that Bert was still in custody and refusing to reveal the name or whereabouts of his boss, Cyndi phoned the police chief in Milltown, telling him she felt sure she could identify the voice of the man if they apprehended him and needed extra verification.

The newspaper Mr. Darby left with the milk a few days later had another article on the ongoing marijuana series. Cyndi began to read.

> Police are hoping to soon have in custody one of the leaders of the group, if not the ringleader himself. Someone associated with our local fire tower has informed police of the last name of a man she believes is one of the suspects. Although that name is unknown to authorities in this area, she believes if the suspected person is apprehended she could make voice identification of him if necessary. The person she referred to is the one who ordered the arson of the two forest plots where recent marijuana raids were carried out.

Jeff phoned that evening, and when Cyndi mentioned it to him, he said gravely, "I'm glad you're public spirited and want to help your new friend's husband, but it may not have been a wise thing to do. Be careful, will you? Stay close to home when you can."

He told her that Lucio was torn up by Juan's death, feeling he should have noticed something different about the boy. Said he'd noticed the faint chicken-coop odor around him and had it been anyone but Juan he would have suspected he was on pot, but decided the odor was associated with Juan's work on a farm.

Then, just as seriously, Jeff said, "I need to see you, Cyndi. Seems like a long time since we were together at the wedding. May I come down in two weeks, about noon that Saturday?"

Cyndi agreed, but had a mixture of anticipation and dread. Because she was very fond of him and they always had fun together, she anticipated being with him, but the feeling that he would press her for an answer regarding her feelings for him made her uneasy.

Her spirits were lifted that evening when Tim phoned. Cyndi's heart skipped a beat when she heard his voice.

"If you're free tonight, will you have supper with me at Bertha's Restaurant? I could pick you up about seven."

Tables at Bertha's were almost all taken, but they found an empty one near the edge of the room. Background music and conversation of the other diners made a pleasant background that Cyndi and Tim hardly noticed as their eyes met across the table. Tim looked at her for a long moment, then he smiled, touching her hand with his fingertips.

"Been quite a while since we've eaten together. I've missed you, Cyndi, very much." His voice was low, filled with what she had already seen in his eyes. When she made no reply, he averted his gaze. Then again searching her eyes he added, "I've some good news concerning the mill property . . . You *are* still interested?" He raised his eyebrows questioningly.

Cyndi nodded. Tim reached across the table again and clasped her hand a moment.

"I've arranged for purchase of the property, getting it cheap for unpaid back taxes. Dad's behind me in this, so he sold some woodland he was recently offered an excellent price for and contributed the money to cover most of it.

"The bank's loaning me enough to start renovation on the mill, based on the involvement of some local business people who've agreed to invest in the first phase of building the reconstructed pioneer village."

Tim's eyes were sparkling; a tinge of excitement touched his voice.

"You're very happy about this, aren't you?" Cyndi said, smiling at his obvious joy.

"I'm very pleased that my plan finally seems to be coming together. It'll be great, Cyndi . . . So many youngsters have nothing worthwhile to do with their free time—adults too. I especially want to acquaint the kids with the wonders of nature and evidences of the generations who lived in this area long before we came.

"Our main problem," he continued, "will be to prevent vandalism once we make it public. We'll have to make plain to people who come here that they may look and touch but not dig or take. Any relics located here need to be retrieved carefully and notes made on their location so the information isn't lost," Tim explained.

Cyndi said nothing about the "we" in his comments but offered, "I appreciated the notations in your collection . . . made it extra interesting."

"Right, otherwise the things are just isolated items with no record of their connection to the life of the people who used them."

Cyndi shared Tim's exuberance over his subject as they continued the discussion over their meal. Finishing one of Bertha's special blueberry tarts, Tim said, "The archaeologist from Glenn Black is coming down a week from Saturday to take her advance look at the place. Want to come along?"

"Yes, I'd—oh, I'm sorry, Tim, I can't. I've promised to be with Jeff that day. I'm really sorry."

Tim's expression was as though he'd been struck. He stared speechlessly for a fraction of a second; then Cyndi saw a shadow of pain in his eyes just before he dropped his gaze.

He looked up almost immediately, clearing his throat, his voice sounding jagged as he said, "I see . . . well, possibly I'll see you sometime after that . . . bring you up-to-date or something."

His eyes held an expression of stunned hurt; Cyndi felt miserable.

Tim pushed his chair back, "Let's go, okay?"

Conversation was strained on the drive home. Her heart aching, yet not knowing what to do about it, Cyndi was glad when Tim said good-night at her door and drove away, spinning the van's wheels on the gravel in Grandpa's drive as he pulled out.

The weather turned increasingly cold the next week, unusually so for that time of year. When Cyndi talked to Grandpa on the phone, he urged her to start filling the kitchen-window bird feeder from the metal can in the barn.

The next week and a half Cyndi spent an extra amount of time praying, especially before finally falling asleep the night prior to Jeff's expected visit.

She awoke before dawn on that day and padded downstairs on bare feet, her robe unfastened. Snapping on the kitchen light, she started coffee. While it brewed she stepped out onto the back porch. Faint moonlight lingered, but in the distance a tinge of color touched the horizon.

The floorboards felt rough and cold to her feet. She fastened her robe, then opened the screen door and went down a step, breathing in the cold air.

The resident owl hooted softly in the tall tree at the corner of the yard. She heard the sound of ducks high and far away, their calls becoming louder and louder, then softer again as they flew overhead and passed by.

Cyndi went back inside, poured coffee at the table, and pulled Grandpa's Bible toward her from where she'd left it the night before.

Let not your heart be troubled. On and on she read until

turmoil left her thoughts and she felt calm and sure.

A soft thud outside the window caught her attention and she saw daylight breaking over the land. Cyndi smiled at the industrious bluejay who had lighted on the feeder and now rat-a-tat-tatted a sunflower seed open.

Pushing back her tousled hair, Cyndi poured more coffee, scrambled some eggs, and made toast. By eleven o'clock she was ready for Jeff's arrival, with chicken and potatoes roasting in the oven, rolls rising, and salad crisping in the refrigerator.

Their meal at the kitchen table was pleasant but with an underlying tension in the atmosphere and in Jeff's eyes building up to the inevitable. As she was serving dessert, he stood and put his arms around her.

"I want you to know that I love you, Cyndi. I planned to wait until Thanksgiving to tell you this . . . I've ordered a ring . . . but my heart feels like it will burst if I don't tell you now!"

Gently she disengaged his arms and he saw in her eyes his answer. Very quietly, his arms at his sides, he said hoarsely, "There's someone else, isn't there?"

Mutely Cyndi nodded, putting her hand out in a comforting gesture to touch his arm.

The delicious peach cobbler was tasteless to both of them, like cardboard in their mouths. Jeff refused a second cup of coffee, leaving soon afterward.

Two weeks later the mailbox along the road at the end of the drive held a letter addressed to her on an envelope of finest bond:

Dear Cyndi,

Thanks for the lovely dinner; it was sweet and thoughtful of you to prepare it for me.

My heart aches when I realize that you will never be my wife . . . Yet there is lingering joy, too, because of knowing you. I thank our God for that.

I will always love you, though in a different capacity (as soon as I can convince myself of the fact that you are not to be mine).

I will never forget you.

Jeff

22

Cynthia had seen Tim at church the Sunday following the supper at Bertha's. He nodded from across the room but made no move to speak with her. Nor did she hear from him during the following weeks.

Tempted to phone him, she started to dial several times—but then decided not to.

She wanted to tell him about the breaking of her relationship with Jeff, but was afraid he might not readily forgive the pain she'd caused when she didn't reassure him the last time they were together.

David wrote to say he was to visit a friend's home over Thanksgiving weekend and Grandpa phoned urging her to come to his sister's; he'd pay the plane fare. She thanked him, but declined, instead spending Thanksgiving day in the tower with a sack lunch, feeling sorry for herself.

Several times during the morning she heard a truck motor and the whirring roar of a chainsaw. She tried to think of who might be working in the forest on a holiday.

Shortly after two o'clock when she returned to the tower, her feet crunching on drifts of dry leaves, she saw a man skulking among the trees. When he became aware she had seen him, he ducked into the underbrush.

Sure hope timber isn't being stolen, she fretted, feeling uneasy and deciding to report her suspicion the next day. She wondered at the heavy odor of gasoline but supposed it must be lingering from the chainsaws she'd heard earlier.

The breeze that had been blowing was changing into a chilly wind, developing funnels that occasionally swirled leaves all the way up to the tower windows.

Cyndi turned on the little portable heater and went back to her drawing. She laid that aside after awhile, deciding to read. But from listening to the wind in the cozy warmth of the cabin, she was soon asleep, her head resting against the window.

She wakened with a start when her book slipped from the sill, hitting the floor with a thud. A glance out the window brought her to her feet, a scream to her lips. "Fire!"

Not fire in the distance this time, not a wisp of haze on the horizon, but flames nearby. Red and yellow flames grasped at trees, swallowing bushes whole. Cyndi's body felt like lead as she moved, realizing the fire was only a few hundred yards away.

It seemed to her that she was moving in slow motion as she tried to hurry to the radio. Her horrified eyes saw that the fire was everywhere around her—a complete ring.

And no one's in the towers because of the holiday! her mind screamed. Moving from the radio her hand frantically grabbed for the phone, her finger instinctively dialing Tim's home number.

Waiting for him to answer, she looked again out the windows.

"It's a doughnut of fire, Tim!" she gasped frantically when he answered. "There's a fire all around the edge of the field."

"Where are you? Who's helping you?"

"I'm in the tower. No one's here. I'm alone!" she cried, her voice becoming high and on the verge of a thin scream of fear.

"Oh, Tim! There's no way to get out of the clearing!"

Tim took command immediately. "Alert everyone you

can and try to stay calm—I'll come for you!" he shouted before slamming down the receiver.

Her fingers trembling, Cyndi began dialing, passing on the location information. She tried to stay calm, but fear clutched at her throat.

The next ten minutes seemed like hours to Cyndi.

Will they never get here! her frantic thoughts asked over and over as she watched the wind blowing leaping flames close against the clearing on the south and west. The fire was fanned into fury on the rest of the perimeter by drafts the fire itself was creating.

Sirens were approaching now but already the heat was reaching the cabin high above the treetops. Cyndi rushed to turn off the heater and pull open a window. But the blast of extra heat caused her to slam it shut again.

"How can Tim or a fire truck possibly get through this fire?" she worried aloud. "It seems to extend so far out!" Her fear was mounting, almost causing her to rush down the stairs and across the clearing to her car. But the flames were approaching so close to it that she knew the metal would probably be too hot to touch.

"Is it my time to die, Lord?" she whispered, tears of emotion flooding her eyes. "Am I to die in such a horrible way?"

Just then the radio crackled, "Redbud! Redbud! Cyndi, this is Tim! Are you there?"

"Yes, Tim, yes! Are you almost here?"

"Be calm, Cyndi, and listen carefully. We can't reach you by the roads. Someone's blocked them with felled trees; we have no equipment here to move them.

"Hold on now and listen. Are you all right?"

"Yes, so far," she answered, her voice quavering. "But it's getting awfully hot and the fire's almost reached my car!"

"Okay. Trust God and pray . . . I'm going for the helicopter—already on the way in fact. When you see me approaching, open the window. We'll lower a rope with a harness; fasten it tightly around you beneath your arms, hang on to the rope and shut your eyes. Got it?"

"Yes," Cyndi said, tears spilling down her cheeks. "Please hurry, Ace! Please hurry . . . I don't want to die yet."

"I'll be there! Pray, Cyndi, pray!"

There was silence then for a while except for the roaring and crackling of the fire below.

Then she heard more sirens approaching in the distance as more fire units responded from surrounding areas. Glancing down, she saw the little outhouse enveloped in fire a moment before she noticed the leaping flames beginning to close around her car.

Cyndi watched in the hypnotic fascination of terror as the car was devoured by the greedy flashing red and yellow tongues. In another few moments the intense heat pressed the gas tank and it exploded with a roar.

Cyndi fell to the floor as flames shot higher into the air joined by fragments of metal.

Terror mounting, her body shaking with sobs of fear, she pulled herself up to peek over the windowsill.

She could barely see the frame of her demolished car through the flames and black smoke boiling around it. Acrid fumes, their odor filled with gas, oil, burning plastics, and forest were seeping more and more into the cabin, making breathing increasingly difficult. Cyndi's eyes burned and watered; her throat felt parched.

Pulling her partially empty canteen from her tote, she swallowed a large gulp, then stopped, remembering what was to come.

When Tim comes with the helicopter, I'll have to open a window. How will I be able to stand it? she said to herself, fear twisting her in its grasp.

"Lord, what shall I do?" she prayed aloud. "Please show me what to do!"

Hands shaking, she wet her fingertips from the canteen,

tipping it cautiously so as not to spill any of the precious liquid. Moistening her parched lips, she carefully screwed the lid back in place.

Cyndi strained to see through the thick fog surrounding her high cabin, feeling completely isolated—nothing but angry, ugly red-yellow flames as far as she could see. Smoke from the fire had turned the bright afternoon into the gloom of night.

Even if Tim gets here, how will he be able to find the tower in the heavy smoke? she wondered, panic mounting.

"Lord Jesus, show me; what shall I do?" she prayed again. In the same instant Cyndi thought she heard a distant "chop-chop-chop." Glancing down at the canteen in her hand, an idea formed in her mind as she also remembered her flashlight.

She couldn't hear the "chop-chop" now and knew it may have been her imagination.

Grabbing her long scarf from the hook on the wall above the trapdoor, Cyndi folded the soft wool to half its length, put it on the chair and carefully soaked the center portion with the water remaining in the canteen.

Positioning the wet area of the material over her mouth and nose she fumbled through her tote with her other hand for her sketch pencil. Then she hurriedly folded the scarf ends firmly at the back of her head, her trembling fingers utilizing the pencil to force holes through the bulky weave, using it as a straight pin to hold the scarf in place.

Certain she again heard the faint chopping sound above the roaring and cracking of the flames, Cyndi jabbed her arms into her nylon jacket, zipping it to her chin. Hurriedly pulling the hood up over the lump of scarf, she tied it close around her face with the drawstring.

Then grabbing her long flashlight, she threw open a window and shone the beam straight up.

Dark gray smoke blew in around her; even through the

scarf she gasped. Intense heat struck her hands and the small portion of uncovered face around her eyes and forehead. Her eyes watered so she could hardly hold them open.

Cyndi leaned out of the window, searching the darkness for some sign of assurance, her throat aching with tears of fear.

She saw it when a gust of wind blew the dense smoke aside for a moment—in the sky, a tiny flashing red light.

As it drew closer she noticed a smaller, steady red light accompanying the flashing one, as well as a green one. The "chop-chop-chop" of the helicopter's rotor blades was definite now, getting louder and louder.

"Thank you, Lord," Cyndi prayed with relief. "Thank you." In her excitement she almost dropped the flashlight from her hand, now numb from gripping it so tightly.

Cyndi peered through the murkiness, all at once discerning the copter's cabin. Then the rotating blades momentarily appeared above it when the smoke shifted again.

The rotor sounds were deafening now and the enormity of the task of reaching the safety of that cabin from this one overwhelmed her.

Suddenly, from the wall of smoke, Cyndi saw the helicopter burst into definite outline—it was coming fast.

Tilted forward, its tail rotor sticking out behind, it stopped abruptly and hung stationary, above and to one side of the tower.

The rotating red light on its top filled the plastic-bubble cabin with a weird glow. In its eerieness Cyndi saw a hand wave, a door open, an object begin to descend.

"The harness!" she realized. "How will Tim ever get it to the window? The wind's too wild—I know it is!" she worried.

But slowly, surely it descended, the pilot maneuvering carefully to accommodate the force of the currents from the fire and the rotors.

All at once the harness loomed exactly opposite Cyndi, only about a yard away. Dropping the flashlight to the floor, she gripped the side of the window frame with one hand, then reached out toward the harness . . . farther . . . farther.

"It's too far!" she screamed into the scarf muffling her voice. "I can't reach it!"

Slowly it inched toward her. Again she stretched outward, straining to grab it.

Farther and farther her body moved out over the windowsill until only her thighs were holding her there, the sill felt as though it was cutting into them.

Great sobs rose in Cyndi's throat as her fingertips touched the harness. It slipped away from her grasp as the searing wind shifted and swirled around her high perch. Almost plummeting out the window to the ground far below, she screamed in terror and jerked herself backward, hands flailing to finally grasp the window's edge.

Her strength almost gone, Cyndi slid to the floor trying to catch her breath, inhaling in great gulps through her painful throat.

In disbelief, she watched the harness move quickly upward and disappear in the cloud of smoke.

"Don't leave me, Ace! Please, don't leave me," she moaned as she crawled back to the window and pulled herself up.

The helicopter was no longer in sight. A sense of dull desolation swept over her as she stared at the horrible spectacle below.

This must be what hell looks like, she thought, her head dropping forward, her chin against her chest as she sobbed despondently huddled on the floor.

Cyndi seemed to hear a voice then, soft and comforting, "Fear thou not, for I am with thee. I am thy God; I will not forsake thee."

At the same moment she became aware that the "chop-

chop-chop" of the rotors was again present, even louder than before. The sound crashed around her, making the little fire tower cabin vibrate on its spindly legs.

Cyndi lifted her head, listening intently through the roar, certain something had scraped on the metal roof. Abruptly something banged against the window next to the open one, cracking it with a loud snapping sound.

"The harness! It's the harness!" She scrambled up to the window, gripped its edge with one hand and reached out with the other to grab the harness that moved back and forth across the shattered pane.

When she had it firmly in hand, the rope suddenly became slack so she could pull it inside. The roaring of the rotor engine decreased.

"Cyndi!" The shout came from above. Cyndi stuck her head out the window into the swirling smoke and debris.

Directly above her the huge blades were slowly rotating. Gazing in awe at the lazily whirling blades, she realized Ace had actually set the craft down on the tiny roof.

"Cyndi! Can you hear me?"

"Yes! Yes! I have the harness!" she yelled, pulling the scarf up off her mouth momentarily so her voice could be heard.

"When you have it on and fastened securely, yank three times on the line!"

"Okay. Yank three times!" she repeated.

Working as quickly as she could with her trembling hands, gasping for breath through her now almost dry scarf, Cyndi secured herself and yanked on the line.

Tim's voice came again. "Straddle the windowsill—we'll pull you up to the roof!"

Breathless now, smoke searing her throat, she jerked three times more, stuck one leg out the window and, gripping the rope tightly with one hand, grasped the window edge with the other and clenched her burning eyes shut.

Immediately she was lifted upward, her foot dragging over the sill skinning her ankle. Then strong hands grasped her wrists and pulled her over the roof's edge. A moment later she felt herself being shoved through the copter's door, then wedged between two people.

Cyndi couldn't seem to open her eyes. Her breath tore at her throat in jagged gulps as the roar of the motor increased.

23

Cynthia knew the scarf had been pulled from her face and something cool pressed over her mouth and nose. Now she was in a place of deep quiet, wanting only to sleep. Vaguely she heard a voice she recognized as Bill's from Bluebird tower.

"She'll be all right . . . just smoke inhalation and a bad scare."

Forcing her eyes open, she saw Tim's face gazing anxiously at her. Behind his head, through the copter's bubble, she could see the Nichols' house. Reaching in through the door to snug a blanket around her was Bill.

She formed a weak smile and thank you with lips encompassed by the plastic oxygen mask.

With difficulty she turned her head back to Tim to thank him, too, but her eyes drifted shut.

Cyndi woke to find herself in an unfamiliar bedroom. She lay fully clothed, except for her shoes, on a four-poster bed under a softly quilted comforter. A shaded lamp on a round, skirted bedside table revealed a glass and small pitcher of ice water, a note propped against them:

> You're in the guest room at our home.
> So thankful you're all right.
> Sleep as long as you like.
>
> Tim and Dad

Relieved, Cyndi snuggled back under the comforter's

fluffy warmth. When she awoke again, the lamp was off, sunlight was flooding beneath a partly raised window shade, and a glass of orange juice had replaced the water pitcher. A pretty comb and brush partially covered another note:

> Bathroom's down the hall to your left.
> Feel free to use Mom's robe and my socks that are on the chair by your bed.

The delicious aroma of coffee and frying sausages made her realize how hungry she was when she opened the bedroom door.

A short time later Cyndi emerged from the bathroom feeling rested and refreshed. The blue flannel robe was wrapped softly around her and heavy white socks bunched ahead of her toes as she found her way to the kitchen.

A sudden sense of warm belonging flooded over her when Mr. Nichols looked up, saying, "Well, here's our girl, Ace."

Spatula in hand, Tim turned his tall, slim frame from the stove to smile at her. His eyes betrayed his emotions, but he said nothing, turning back to the stove. When he poured batter on the hot griddle, the delicious smell of pancakes mingled with those of the coffee and sausages, and Cyndi could hardly wait to eat.

During breakfast the men urged her to be their guest for a few days. Because no one had felt like having a traditional Thanksgiving meal the previous day, they decided to take the turkey from the freezer and plan a festive meal for Sunday. They each felt they had much to thank God for.

The weather became frosty cold with a scattering of snow that night. Tim drove his yellow van to the Carlson house to care for the chickens and check the bird feeders. Returning home he filled theirs and scattered corn around the lilac bush that stood about forty feet from the back door.

Following breakfast the next morning, Tim handed her

one of his jackets. "I want to show you something outside—hurry!"

A thin layer of white covered the lawn. Tim pointed and Cyndi saw under the lilac bush a beautiful, large male pheasant.

Slowly they moved closer, but as they approached, he rose with a great flutter of wings.

"What a beauty!" Tim exclaimed.

"A nice addition to a perfect visit," Cyndi added softly.

Saturday Tim went into Milltown for cranberry sauce and mincemeat, bringing a newspaper back with him. He handed it to Cyndi, so she browsed through it while he went out to do his chores.

> The big fire that threatened the life of local firefighter Cynthia Carlson was evidently set to silence her in connection with the recent marijuana investigation. A truck filled with empty five-gallon gas cans, found stalled on the old Parson blacktop road during the fire, was traced to Carlton Potter of Chicago, a known racketeer. Police report it is the same vehicle driven by Bertell Jones at his recent arrest on charges of transporting large amounts of marijuana.
>
> Jones is at present free on bond. His sentencing may be shortened due to his current cooperation with law enforcement agencies. At his suggestion, State Troopers apprehended Potter on the farm occupied by Jones' family, where he had gone to meet a plane preparing to remove another large cache of the dried weed.
>
> According to Jones, Potter had, at an earlier date, checked from the Redbud fire tower with powerful binoculars to ascertain that the two arsoned forest plots could not be seen from that vantage point.
>
> Authorities estimate the street value of the high-grade marijuana taken in recent raids to be well over a million dollars. Local banker, Joseph Zodest, who re-

cently acquired the farm on which Potter was apprehended, has been cleared of any involvement.

The two days at the Nichols' home passed swiftly for Cyndi. Then, Sunday morning, Tim and his dad drove her home, waiting while she dressed for church.

Entering the sanctuary, Cyndi saw Sally and Bert, with Samantha between them. She rushed forward to greet them. Two rows ahead were a man and his son. Tim introduced them as Joseph and Dan Zodest.

He told Cyndi in a whisper as they seated themselves behind the pair that Dan blamed himself for Juan's death and was very repentant, not only about that but because he was living without ever giving God a thought.

"He and his dad both seem close to making a commitment to the Lord," Tim added.

The following weeks brought high, jagged cumulus clouds which dissipated quickly on the currents. The air became colder, and more often now Cyndi could enjoy the sight of falling snow.

Both David and Grandpa planned to be there for Christmas, so she became happily immersed in plans for their coming. Bright-colored wrapping paper splayed over the end of her bed. Strings of holiday lights and tinsel lay in piles on the sofa beside boxes of ornaments ready for the tree.

"I'll cut a tree from our land and bring it over . . . help you set it up," Tim had offered during one of their phone conversations.

Because he was extending the area of helicopter reconnaissance now, continuing Bill's training in sighting and rescue work, Cyndi didn't have to spend time in the tower very often.

Daily the Carlson house was filled with aromas of chocolate and spices from the cookies and pies being prepared for the freezer and candies filling trimmed jars and boxes in the pantry.

Holiday breads and rolls bursting with fruit and nuts, jellies and candied citrus peels were cooling on racks covering every available space in the kitchen the afternoon Tim arrived with the tree.

Chickadees and other birds feasted at the snow-topped window feeder. Their colorful movements just outside the pane delighted Cyndi.

"How about some coffee and fresh rolls?" she asked Tim a few minutes later as he helped her stabilize the prickly tree in its stand.

"Sounds great," Tim agreed. "Would you like a drive out to the mill and a short hike afterward? It's beautiful outside."

"I'd love to, Tim," she answered, her heart filled with the sincere love she held for him—love she was afraid he might no longer want.

Although he had continued to be a pleasant, helpful friend since her rescue from the fire, he had been reserved in his attitude toward her. She wondered if he thought she and Jeff were making marriage plans. She'd never told him otherwise. But the feeling she had for Tim now was beyond anything she had felt for Jeff or even Mark. She had finally discovered the vast difference between true love and infatuation.

Later, as the van bumped them over the frozen dirt road from the blacktop to the mill, Cyndi said, "I'm not seeing Jeff anymore . . . We're just friends."

"Are you sure, Cyndi?"

"Yes, Tim, I'm sure," she replied softly, the tenderness in her heart toward him almost overwhelming her.

"Good," he said reaching for her hand, squeezing it momentarily. "I'm your friend, too . . . more than I could possibly put into words."

Cyndi's heart seemed to shrivel inside her.

My friend? she thought as the van stopped. *Is that all he wants from me now, just friendship? Maybe it's all for the best somehow.*

The best? her senses shouted inside her head. *How can it ever be "the best" when my heart is breaking?*

Because she just sat there, Tim came around to open her door. Confused and dejected, she stepped down from the van into a snowy wonderland her sad eyes hadn't been noticing.

The call of a cardinal brought her gaze upward. Dark skeletons of leafless trees stretched above her; softly falling puffs of snow dislodged by the red plumaged bird settling on a limb touched her face.

Cyndi brushed them away with her mittened hand, removing at the same time the tears threatening to slip from the corners of her eyes. Evidently not noticing, Tim reached out and grasped her other hand. They walked in silence through the beautiful white landscape toward the mill.

They found the stream frozen along its edges, a red-winged blackbird roosting among the dried cattails in the twilight.

Several tiny chickadees, their black caps dark against their gray-white suits, perched on twigs of a barberry bush, searching even at this late hour for insect eggs.

Cyndi listened with saddened interest as Tim shared new ideas and progress regarding plans for this long-cared-about piece of land.

The paths they walked were almost obliterated by snow and fallen leaves, but the way had become familiar like an old friend.

Tim had been silent for a while now as they crunched along. Twilight had flowed into early darkness; the moon was rising, bright and full.

As they turned back to the path leading to the van, the fields began to sparkle in the moonlight.

Every stalk and twig threw a dark shadow on the glittering snow. The forest edge formed a dark wall around the scene, with the soaring rock slab shimmering above the silvered, icy stream.

Unable to bear the silence with her heartache, trying to think of some subject for conversation, Cyndi said, "I got a letter from Jennifer today. She and Lucio are very happy together. Although Juan's tragedy followed so closely, I thought their wedding was beautiful and happy."

Tim nodded. "There's a wedding I would be happy to attend—about the time the apple trees blossom next spring maybe."

"Oh, whose?" Cyndi asked, not really caring.

"Ours," Tim said gently, his voice deep with feeling.

"Ours?" Cyndi questioned softly, her breath catching in her throat.

"Ours—yours, Cyndi, and mine." Turning toward her, Tim held out his arms, hope shining in his eyes. "Will you be my wife?"

Cyndi stepped forward and snuggled against his chest. "Ours," she whispered, lifting her face for his kiss. "Yes, Tim, I will. Apple blossom time will be perfect."

As he lowered his head to hers, she heard his whispered, "Thank you, Lord."